Get Well
Soon Chuck
We need you Back
on the racetrack!

The Color of Coffee
of My

The Story of a White Boy and a Black Man

R.P. HEINZ

authorHOUSE®

AuthorHouse™
1663 Liberty Drive
Bloomington, IN 47403
www.authorhouse.com
Phone: 1 (800) 839-8640

Published by AuthorHouse   06/14/2017

ISBN: 978-1-5246-9616-0 (sc)
ISBN: 978-1-5246-9614-6 (hc)
ISBN: 978-1-5246-9615-3 (e)

Library of Congress Control Number: 2017909314

Print information available on the last page.

CONTENTS

Chapter One

LOVE AND MONEY

I reached out to the cheap silver doorknob, but then hesitated, and took in a deep breath instead. Rapping my knuckles on the door would be a waste of time, even though it seemed like the right thing to do. Rehearsing the lines in my head once again, I turned the knob, and eased open the fake wood door. In spite of the bright sunlight shining outside, the room was dark, and I needed to adjust my eyes.

Thick green curtains choked out the daylight by completely covering the windows on either side of the room. I tried, but could not remember, when the musty old drapes had last been opened.

There was a queen bed covered by a dark green comforter that matched the curtains and two faux-Victorian side tables facing me from across the far wall. A small, blue, upholstered chair was on the left side of the bed, and on the right there was a black and white portable television sitting precariously on top of a rolling metal serving tray.

I walked to the chair and sat down. There was a bulge in the bed; a shapeless form crowned by two rumpled pillows where a head would normally be. Next to me, on the side table, were three translucent pill bottles surrounding an ashtray full of twisted cigarette butts. I leaned over to read the typewritten label on one of the half empty bottles, but the words were printed in a language I did not understand.

"Mom?" I whispered.

"Mom?"

The blanket wrinkled; the bulge moved.

"Mom, can I talk to you?"

A thin, pale, hand emerged and removed the pillow covering her face. Part of her head was now showing; it was a muss of black and gray hair, below which a pasty white nose stuck out just above the lip of the covers.

"What? What do you want?" She mumbled.

"It's Stevie Mom, I wanted to tell you something."

"What! What is it? What do you want?"

Her eyes opened, about halfway, and I remembered for just that moment how vibrant she had once been. She was always my biggest fan, my leading supporter, and the only one interested in my few noteworthy achievements.

"I, I, just wanted to tell you Mom; I'm quitting the baseball team."

"Mmmph, what?"

"I'm quitting; baseball. I'm going to work instead. I got a job Mom. I need the money. I just wanted to let you know 'cause you told me I was good at it, and I should stick with it."

"Umm, tha's fine dear, have a good time."

"You understand Mom? I'm never playin' baseball again."

"Ok honey, turn the lights out now, Mom's gonna go back to sleep."

She grabbed the discarded pillow and pulled it back up onto her head, thus signaling the end of our brief conversation.

I stood up, listened to her breathing for a moment, turned, and walked away. As I passed the tall wooden dresser that sat by the doorway exit, I glanced down at the silver dish that sat on top of it. I removed the seventy-five cents in change that was resting there and left the room.

As I closed the door behind me I paused, feeling as though I had left something behind in that dreary room, but I could not think of what it was, so I moved on.

Outside, in the hallway, I looked down at the three silver coins in the palm of my hand. I knew then, that I could learn to live without my mother's love, but I also knew, I could not live without the money.

*****

And there it was: lying in its filthy bed, right in front of me. The pot at the end of a foul, colorless rainbow: three quarters, a nickel, and two pennies. Hidden by the bobby pins, potato chip bags, dirty diapers, soiled Kleenex, bottle caps, used and unused prophylactics, unidentified pills, Lucky Strike cigarettes, and assorted other human flotsam left beneath the back seat of a 1962 Chevrolet Impala sedan. It was mine to keep, an unwritten law of the automobile cleaning profession otherwise known as car detailing. If you could stomach cleaning up the worst evidence of human behavior, you could keep anything of value that came with it.

And what a value that eighty-two cents enjoyed back in 1966. I thought, before pocketing the cash, what I would do with those long lost coins. Three precious gallons of gas for my old ford? Five nauseating lunches at the school cafeteria, or better yet, five delicious McDonald's cheeseburgers? Find seventeen cents more, and I might find someone old enough to buy me a six-pack of beer Friday to share with my buddy Jack for our big night out. The opportunities seemed endless.

It was the year that my life, like our television, would turn from a fuzzy black and white to full living color. I was only sixteen at the time, so I was not able not to grasp the tumultuous events of the late 1960's that were beginning to churn all around me. The clothes we wore, the language we used, our attitudes towards sex, drugs, and music; everything was about to change, including the innocence I had so stubbornly clung to.

I was leaning in through the aging Chevy's back door over the area that held the now-removed back seat, with my commercial wet/dry vacuum in hand. Shirtless, I was wearing only a pair of filthy old blue jeans and my well worn P.F. Flyer tennis shoes as the sweat dripped off my forehead and down onto the rear carpets that I had yet to clean. It was ninety-eight degrees out, a scorching summer day in Southern California; the same, really, as every other day there in the summertime. Fullerton, where I had lived up until that time, was a small community just a few miles too far inland to enjoy the cooling coastal breezes of the Pacific Ocean. We suffered instead from the inversion layer of heat and smog that collected along the base of the San Bernardino Mountains every year, making life miserable for those of us who worked outdoors.

There were, back then, still no smog rules of any consequence in California so the cars and factories belched out the purest black pollutants money could buy. Sometimes, the smog was so thick I wasn't able to see across the street. Many of those days I would start coughing about three o'clock in the afternoon and wheeze all night long. The only relief I had came from the cheap window air conditioner in our house that my father had bartered for as a down payment on a 1958 Buick he sold to a "friend" back when he owned his used car dealership.

As I freed the coins from the rubble under the seat and safely tucked them away in my denim pocket, I spotted a small plastic toy that was partially hidden by a yellowed old dry cleaning ticket. I wondered for a moment if the child it belonged to was sad to have lost it, or if the child was even a child anymore. It was a miniature Hawaiian surfer with a lei around his neck; he and his little surfboard were painted a rubberized blue and his arms stretched out as he looked for the perfect balance while riding his imaginary wave. I picked it up and inspected it more closely. He was smiling, having a good time, and my thoughts ran to what other teenage boys might be doing that day, and to what I should have been doing instead of cleaning up the worst part of this shitty old car: lounging on the warm sands of nearby Newport Beach.

It was just last week when I called in sick instead of working that day, and I can recall every delicious moment. I knew there would not be another one like it for a very long time.

Jack and I hitchhiked the twenty miles down Harbor Boulevard needing only two rides, the last from a friendly surfer who thumbed us into the back of his 1956 Ford pickup truck. We then spent the day bodysurfing and carefully scrutinizing the young girls who seemed to enjoy showing off the best parts of their blossoming womanhood. After sponging hot dogs and a Coke off of a friendly tourist family, we took our pink bodies back to the streets for another borrowed ride home.

Shaking myself out of that pleasant daydream, I tossed the happy little surfer out of the open car door and brought myself back to reality.

I drew myself backward and out of the car to choke up a nice-size chunk of sulfur dioxide I hocked out about ten feet behind me in the form of a "lugie"; as my brother, Tom, named any good-size chunk of spittle. What a crappie job, I thought, looking at my grimy hands; how in hell did I get here? Was I destined to do this boring work for the rest of my life? I had no idea at the time how things were about to change.

My job, car detailing, despite what one might think, was a very structured craft: You would start by sponging clean the headliner as everything dripped back down. Sponge or scrub it with your mix of upholstery soap, water, and a dash of TSP stain remover. Pull the seats out, a chore much harder than you may think, scrub them with the same mixture, vacuum, rinse, and vacuum again. Scrub the door panels, shampoo the carpets, vacuum again, and then clean underneath the seats. Scrub the trunk, clean the windows, and you're finished.

The job took about two hours, depending on the sanitary habits of the previous owner, and earned me the whopping sum of $4.25 per job. It *was*, after all, 1966, and I, Steven Reilly, *was,* after all, only sixteen years old. This had been my lot in life over the last two years. I'd had it easy until, at the age of fourteen, Benjamin C. Reilly, my dad, announced that his used car business was closing, we were broke, and the kids would, instead of getting an allowance every week, now have to pay him rent every month. This was an unexpected blow that my twenty-one-year-old sister Linda took immediate exception to by announcing that she was leaving home and moving into her own apartment.

This left my older brother Thomas and I holding the bag of shit our father had just handed to us. My mother was in no position to defend her children's financial rights. A quiet, reserved, woman, she usually deferred to my father in the matters of money. Tall and thin, I took after her much more than my dad in both stature and looks. I will always remember her in my childhood as a beautiful, caring, and good-hearted mother. The pressure of raising three independent kids with a semi-absentee father, however, was too much for her. Mom left us to go to her bedroom in the middle of watching *Bonanza* on television one night and she was rarely ever seen again. I never knew the exact diagnosis, but for me, at ten years old, it was a devastating loss.

Thank God for my brother. He was always the levelheaded one in the family. Only eighteen years old at the time of our father's announcement, he had the uncanny ability to keep his cool under any adverse circumstance. I worried about things; Tom fixed them.

"How are we going to make it without any cash?" I asked him. "I need spending money and I sure can't pay Pop any rent. Holy shit, I'm fourteen years old!"

"Look," he told me, "let me figure this out, Stevie, I'll come up with something."

Things didn't seem so bad for Tom as he had a job cleaning cars part time while he attended school. I was in the eighth grade, just trying my best to be a semi-normal kid.

Later in the week, Tom pulled up in front of St. Patrick's Elementary School to pick me up after class and save me the five blocks of walking to get home. Tom drove a gorgeous metallic green 1960 two-door Pontiac Bonneville that he had really "cherried" out. It had a Hurst shifter and tuck and roll upholstery, but best of all, he'd installed a portable record player under the dash that was suspended by four tiny springs. In theory, this allowed the miniature turntable to absorb road vibration, thus allowing the needle to stay accurately in the grooves of the record. This, in the age just before the eight-track tape player, was the ultimate cool accessory.

Tom turned the volume down on Ray Charles, who was crooning "Georgia on My Mind" through the car's reverb stereo speakers as I settled into the passenger seat.

"I think I got a deal for ya, kid," he began, "I cut a deal with Pop. He went to work for Doug Schultz Chevrolet up in Whittier as the used car manager. He says if I can get the equipment, I can clean all the cars for him, you know, start my own detail business. The guy I work for now, Whitey, threw in the towel and said I could have his stuff for two hundred dollars and a bottle of Wild Turkey. The old guy that owns the gas station where Whitey's shop is says I can stay there for fifty bucks a month when Whitey leaves. I figure you get outta school in a couple of weeks so you could work full-time during the summer and part time during the school year. The money should be good, it's piecework; you know, commission. You get paid for the work you do."

Thus began my automotive detailing career. For the next two summers I worked five and a half days a week, no vacation, and during the school year I worked three hours after class plus nine on Saturdays. My specialty was cleaning interiors, but Tom taught me all the other skills as well. I learned to polish, wax, steam-clean, and paint engines to look like new. Our mission was to turn every shitty old used car into a fresh, glistening pre-owned automobile.

Tom, I admit, worked harder than I did. Cleaning interiors was backbreaking work, but polishing cars was even worse. In those days you used an electric buffing machine that powered a metal rotary disk with a soft pad attached to it that rubbed in, at high speed, the commercial polish we squirted all over the car. The machine weighed over twenty pounds, but by the end of the day, it felt like a hundred. Polish three to five cars a day, including chrome and windows, plus wax, and you really earned your money.

This enterprise worked reasonably well, and Reilly Detail made it through the next year and a half. Tom and I would be able to pay our rent to Pop and still have enough cash left over to meet our basic needs. The downside was that the work schedule left no time for me to hang out with friends, and I became somewhat of a social outcast. While many of the other kids were out having fun, I was working, or spending what little spare time I had doing homework.

It was an evolving time for me, as I graduated from grammar school and moved on to attend the very Catholic private high school St. James, located over on the "good" side of town. The kids who attended St. James were pretty well off, as it was expensive to go there. Most of them came from very successful Catholic families. I was the exception to that rule, as we lived on the edgier west side of town, where the working class lived in their three-bedroom, two-bath, "little-pink" houses.

The only demand my mom ever made of Pop was that her kids go to Catholic school. My grandmother Reilly was a very religious person, and I was sure Mom insisted more out of an obligation to her than an overarching desire to turn us all of us kids into pious Catholics. Rumor had it, as told by my brother, that Pop had given the good priests of St. James a late-model Chevrolet van he had taken as a trade in exchange for my high school education. Tom told me it had been in a terrible accident and that Pop had gotten it for next to nothing. It must have been true, as he never had that much cash on hand and, even if he did, the deal maker in him would never part with it unless a serious horse trade had taken place.

*****

I was by then a sophomore in high school; I had walkin'-around money, summer was just around the corner, and with my newly won drivers license I was able to find myself a car. It was a beauty, a cream puff, and best of all: it ran. I bought it for eighty-two dollars' worth of cleaning dirty interiors but it was worth every penny. It was a 1954 Ford two-door, overhead valve, V-8 with a three-speed shift on the column. It looked as though it had been painted bright blue with a brush by a former owner, but to my eyes it was freedom, and I was able to cut the umbilical cord of transportation Tom and I shared.

Our routine was broken the summer after my sophomore year when Tom took me aside one day at work. He had an unusually serious expression on his face as he slid into the back seat of the 1959 Buick Invicta I was in the middle of cleaning.

"We need to talk," he said, "Things look like they're gonna change. The army is after me because I let too many classes drop at the junior college. I don't want to get caught in the draft; I think they'll shoot my ass off in Vietnam so I'm joining the air force instead."

His statement shocked me; I'd had no idea this drama was taking place; Tom had never mentioned it. I knew all about Vietnam though. We had lost a second cousin there, and I felt some relief that Tom wasn't headed into the quagmire.

"When are you going?"

"Wednesday, next week. I would have told you sooner, but I found out for sure today."

"What about Reilly Detail? I guess I'm out of a job." I said.

"Only if you want. I talked to Pop, and he says if you can handle it he'll keep giving you the work."

"I can't do all that work by myself, you know that."

"Look, Stevie, this could be a great opportunity for you, I know of a guy that needs a full-time job, an experienced guy. You pay me twenty-five dollars a month for a year and you can have the business. Hire this guy and pay him piecework; you know how that works, you get to keep all the profits."

"I'm sixteen," I told him, "what do I know about running a business?"

"Look, butthole, if you don't do it I will find someone else to pay me the cash and then you *will* be out of a job. You know everything about cleaning the cars and I'll show you how to bill the dealers and buy supplies."

"Who is this guy you're talking about?"

"Whitey says he's a good guy, he's been working up at Gussie's detail shop but he's tired of being her slave and wants out. Whitey is bringing him by tomorrow at five. You can meet him then and see if you like him. It's worth a try."

*****

I was nervous the next day, and I had a hard time concentrating on school. I was in Spanish class daydreaming about the prospect of becoming a wealthy teenager when I was brought back to reality by a thick open hand whacking me across the face.

"Mr. Roiley," Father O'Brien brogued at me, "yer badder paid attention from now on or yer gonna speak Spanish out yer rear end cause I be closin' yer mouth permanent-like with me fist."

I took note of the threat, straightened up, and eyed the blackboard that was covered in indecipherable markings. I always thought it strange learning Spanish from a heavily accented Irishman; Spirish, we students called it. Spanish, algebra, and chemistry were the subjects I detested. I performed well enough to pass in those classes, but just barely. English literature, composition, and philosophy had been my favorite subjects. I was always an avid reader; my brother got me started on juvenile books when I was a kid until my high school English teacher, Mr. Watson, graduated me on to the Fitzgerald's and Steinbeck's of the world.

After school that day, I put about scrubbing the insides of an old 1958 four-door Pontiac Chieftain that was a neglected mess. I tore my shirt on the corner of the glove compartment and gashed my forehead open trying to pop the seat out of the back. Dangerous work, I thought, as I tried to clean the blood off of myself with a soapy towel.

I heard Tom talking to someone outside, so I extracted myself from the car and spotted him approaching me with Whitey and another man. Whitey was around five-two and must have weighed all of ninety-eight pounds. He was permanently bent over from years of hard work in a detail shop and I guessed him to be about fifty years old although Tom later told me he was only thirty-five. Most "Whitey's" get that name from their hair; this one got had gotten his name from his skin. He had dirty- brown, unkempt hair long enough to hide part of his bright blue eyes. These features accentuated the translucent whiteness of his face, giving him a ghostly appearance.

Tom turned to me in a very formal manner.

"Stevie, you know Whitey."

"Yeah," I said, "Hi, Whitey, how you been?"

I knew Whitey, as he appeared occasionally to share a beer with Tom after work. I usually opted for an ice-cold Dr. Pepper when they got together, but once in a while they allowed me to enjoy half of a delicious Olympia beer or Brew 102.

Tom turned to the man standing next to Whitey.

"Stevie, this is the man I told you about. I'd like you to meet Herb Jackson. Herb, Stevie."

Now one thing Pop had drilled into all of us was how to greet someone professionally. I remember that when we were children, my father brought my brother and I into the bank when borrowing money, as he often did, and introduced us to the dignified gentleman who might decide his fate. We thought he brought us in for the sympathy we might be able to elicit from the banker, so my brother and I played the part well. We were dressed up in our best Sunday suits, and only after we had practiced our set routine were we allowed to display our ability to greet someone properly.

I used these learned skills by offering my hand to Herb, and upon reciprocation, shook his with a firm grip. My thin white hand disappeared into that big black paw of his. "Pleased to meet you, sir," I said. "I'm Steven Reilly."

The man replied with a big warm toothy grin that is my favorite image of him to this day.

"Pleased to meetcha Steven, Ah'm Herbert, but mostly they call me *the 'Erb*."

Chapter Two

HERB

The fact was; I had never met a black person. Fullerton was ninety-nine percent white, and possibly one percent Hispanic at that time. I don't think they built a wall around the town, but they might as well have. Not in school, not in church, not in the playgrounds, not in the shops downtown, not anywhere I lived; I knew of African-Americans only through books, pictures, and the nightly news.

It had little to do with discrimination, it happened because of migration habits and demographics. Fullerton, and Orange County in which it lay, became settled in the late eighteen hundreds by German and Irish Catholic families moving from the Midwest. Most were farmers, people of the land, who discovered that the climate in California lent itself to year 'round farming versus the six productive months they had back East. Citrus turned out to be the main crop, as rarely did it freeze in Southern California, and Florida was the only real competition. Hence the name: Orange County.

The great Negro migration of the post civil war era passed over the small towns and suburbs of California. These black families were looking for jobs, and they found them in the big cities of Los Angeles and Long Beach, not Orange County. The few Negroes that worked in Orange County when I grew up either lived in the largest city of the time, Santa Ana, or they commuted in for work from neighboring Los Angeles communities.

It was in this context I, never had, and never even thought about, meeting a black man in person.

Herb *was* a black man. He seemed to have a medium build, although it was hard to see beneath all the layers of clothing he wore. The basic uniform in the detail business consisted of a pair of dark blue cotton work pants without a belt, and a long-sleeved light blue work shirt worn over an undershirt suited to one's individual taste. In Herb's case, his shirt was buttoned all the way up to the top, so I observed only the slightest hint of a thick gray T-shirt underneath the collar that begged for a tie that would never be there. His clothes were clean and neat, something I came to expect from Herb at the start of every workday.

Outsized and rough, his hands dwarfed mine and I knew they were those of a worker, not a slacker. Something made me hold on to his handshake longer than I should have; there was a connection between us I could not define.

A handsome man, his skin was the color of weak coffee; but there was no question of his African-American descent due to his very distinctive features. The warm brown eyes of his sparkled when he smiled, and his large but not out-of-place nose flared out wide and strong.

I guessed the man's age at about forty years old. His short-cropped wooly hair was speckled with a hint of gray, and a slight balding in his widow's peak betrayed his age. He was smooth and clean-shaven except for the small wisp of hair some might call a beard he allowed to grow on the bottom of his chin.

Herb's best feature, though, was his smile. There were those exceptionally large white teeth he proudly showed off with a big grin or an energetic laugh. He was one of those people who could light up a room, and I was taken in by that smile before he even began to speak.

"Ah unnerstan' you lookin' for a good man," he began.

"I think so," I replied. "My brother here is joining the air force and if I find the right worker I can take over the business. What detail work can you do?"

"Well, suh, Ah thinks Ah can do it all. Paint motas, *po*-lish" — *always* pronounced like the country— "wax, *in*-ter-ior, Ah does it all.

13

Ah think Ah been doin' detail fo' maybe—twen'y-some yea's. *The 'Erb,* is a *professional* detail man. What 'bout *you*, son, what *you* know?"

As to his speech patterns, I had never heard a man speak with a similar dialect and tone. I grew up thinking black men spoke like Amos and Andy from the comedy show on television back in the fifties and sixties. This program not only stereotyped black men as fools and conniving idiots; it allowed the characters to speak in a guttural slang that exposed a kind of unintelligent laziness in the way they spoke.

Herb was different. His speech never came out as lazy; it was poetry. It was a Southern drawl, more a patois that leaned toward a French or Cajun lilt. Everything he said had a particular rhythm to it. His inflections were intentional, and there was always a sense of meaning to them. I felt you could put his speech to music and have a new hit song every day. I sensed in that first meeting, this man was neither Amos nor Andy; this man knew what he wanted to say.

He always made me feel inferior in that regard. Although I learned more from him than in any speech class I ever attended, I never felt I could measure up to his warm, inviting way of drawing you into his world. My words may have been bigger at times; they were never more meaningful.

Herb's remark put me on the defensive, and I realized this interview was going to be held on a two-way street. As I looked into his eyes, I saw a man seeking a real job, a full-time job. How could he depend on a sixteen-year-old kid to support his family? Doubt wrapped itself around me and I wondered if I was smart enough, old enough, or even confident enough to be this man's boss. He sensed my doubt, but then he smiled that big grin of his and allowed me to think about my answer.

"I have been detailing for almost three years now," I began my pitch. "I *need* the money and I *am* reliable. My brother can tell you I've never missed work. I have steady accounts and I think you could make good money doing piecework for me. I just need to know *you* are reliable. I can't get the work done by myself."

"I unnastan'," he replied. "I jus' wanna make an honest dolla'. Ah woik hard and be here when you need me. Ah give it a try, long as you don' quit on me."

Whitey chipped in, "I worked with him, Stevie. He's a hard worker and a good man; you'd be lucky to have him."

With Whitey's reference, and not any other choices open to me, I agreed. I had no idea what I was getting into; then again, I had nothing to lose.

"I guess we have a deal, then," I told him. "Let's meet here Monday at seven o'clock and get started."

"OK, Chief," he said. "We do got oursel's a deal."

Chapter Three

REILLY DETAIL

Reilly Detail operated out of the site of an ancient Phillips 66 gas station located at the intersection of Fifth and Center Streets in downtown Fullerton. It had, like the neighborhood, seen better days. The bright red paint on the facade had long ago faded and cracked, and I had no money to freshen it up or even to put a sign out. Then again, our customers would never visit the place, so appearance was secondary to functionality. The old gas pumps had been removed many years ago, affording us a generous outdoor work area in addition to four large indoor bays that protected us from the sun. One good-size, private office served as break room, conference room, game room, and my office. A sturdy black sliding scissors gate enclosed the shop at night, keeping our precious equipment safe from predators.

Monday morning Herb, to my relief, arrived right on time. We sat down at the old wooden desk left in the office by some previous entrepreneur and made our plans.

"Our biggest problem is delivery," I began. "I need you to be here working all day, but the cars have to get picked up and delivered in the afternoon. That takes two drivers. I think I can get someone from school to work delivery in the afternoon, that would keep us working together until about three, then I could make deliveries while you finish up here."

"How much work we got?" he asked me.

"My dad says we can get about four cars a day from his place, Doug

Schultz Chevrolet, and I think Sav-Mor Used Cars will give us about one a day. There are a couple of accounts up in Whittier I might get, but I don't think we can handle any more work."

"Ah know a fella needs woik, if'n you want 'im. Good fella, ha'd woiker. Ah figure raght, 'bout fo', five cars a day 'bout all we can do by oursel's."

"Let me talk to the new accounts first," I suggested. "One is a Volkswagen dealer and one is a used car dealer right next door to him. If I can get those accounts, we might hire the guy you know."

The week went better than I'd expected as Herb showed up every day about a half an hour ahead of time. He always looked dapper in a clean uniform, and he was well groomed and ready to go. By the end of the day, however, he and I both appeared as if we had been dragged through the Mojave Desert. A thick coat of car polish, wax, and engine paint of various colors covered us from head to toe. We had three sets of uniforms each, which in my case were three pairs of Levi's jeans and three J. C. Penney blue work shirts. Every two days we loaded up our old open-top washing machine with our dirty laundry, ran it through the double-roller hand-cranked wringer on top, and let it hang up in the office to dry.

Herb was a diligent worker, and he knew what he was doing. As he had told me, he was a true professional. I watched him as he worked, and when I asked him questions, he was patient with me in answering. He took a real pride in his job, and he wanted me to feel the same way. My brother and I only cared about getting the work done as quickly as possible; we were in it for the money, not the end product. Herb, in contrast, was a perfectionist. He allowed no visible wax residue or paint over-spray anywhere. Each car had to pass a rigorous inspection.

Armed with a reference letter from Doug Schultz Chevrolet, I gathered up the courage to approach the two new dealers in Whittier about doing their work for them. To my surprise they both said they would try us out, and I reported back to Herb that he should bring his friend by; we were going to need him.

Chapter Four

THE ASSOCIATE

It was about ten thirty in the morning, Herb was polishing a white 1964 Chevy Bel Air, and I was cleaning the interior of a red 1965 Volkswagen Beetle. I loved the Volkswagens: the interiors were all vinyl with rubber floor mats, so there were no carpets to shampoo and the exteriors had very little chrome to polish. The engines were simple: only one color, black, making them easy to paint. The price the dealers paid us was the same on every car regardless of make or model, so the company profit was considerably more on a Volkswagen than on a Cadillac.

During our morning break we savored a coffee and a Dr. Pepper purchased from the lopsided old catering truck that lumbered in twice a day. Herb knew the proprietor, Hector, or he never would have stopped for such a small operation. I loved the banter between them: it was as creative as it was affable.

Hector: "Hey, Herbie, how come black men don' like black coffee? I lose money on you, *amigo*, you steal all my chu-gar."

Herb: "Yo' coffee so bad I gots to sugar it up. No man drinks yo' coffee black an' lives ta tell 'bout it."

Hector: "Why don't you never buy something to eat, Herbie, the boy don' pay you no money?"

Herb: "I dasn't eat 'cause I got to woik. No man can eats yo' cookin' and woik afterwoids, he be doubled up in mighty pain. I ate once from you and I was inn bafroom fo' a *week*. The chief here don' pay nobody to be inna bafroom."

And so on, until Hector had enough of the heckling and moved on to his next stop, where, hopefully, he would not be as verbally abused.

We leaned against the cracked and faded walls of the office and watched the traffic go by, enjoying the last few moments of our brief recess. Herb looked up; I followed his gaze and saw a car, an old car, turning the corner, and then pulling, ever so slowly, into our driveway.

It was a 1953 Cadillac Coupe de Ville, dark blue, and it sported the widest whitewall tires I had ever seen. It was well cared for and looked to be in perfect condition as it crept into a parking spot on the far side of the lot. We watched in great anticipation as the driver's door eased open. After what seemed like an eternity, a thin, coal-black hand appeared on the top of the door in what looked like a preparatory maneuver for exiting the vehicle.

The frail-looking person inside the car seemed reluctant to leave the comfort of the plush old Cadillac interior. Although it was only a few minutes, it seemed as if it took an hour for the driver to emerge. He was emaciatingly thin. A uniform identical to Herb's hung on him like a badly fitting suit on a scarecrow. He was taller than Herb, about my height, and across his flat wide nose hung reflective sunglasses that covered about half his face. On his head he wore a dark blue corduroy sea captain's hat that had white crossed anchors embroidered across the front.

He sauntered over to us at about the same speed at which he'd removed himself from the car and I was concerned that we might not figure out who he was by quitting time. At last, he made his way to the office, opened the door slowly, ever so slowly, and entered. Taking off his sunglasses, he looked at Herb and drawled out,

"Hallooooo, 'Erb-ert. Is thas the young fella you tol' me 'bout?"

"Yas it is, Speed," Herb replied. "Good ta see ya, man. This here is the chief, Steven. Chief, this here is Speedy Dave Desoto."

At last I came to the to the realization that this was Herb's friend coming to apply for a job. My first impression was that he could have been 103 years old. His skin was the deepest, darkest black I had ever seen. Deep grooves meandered through his cheeks and forehead. A pencil-thin mustache and the long bushy sideburns that framed his face made me think of an ancient Chuck Berry.

Shaking his hand was like grabbing a skinny leather glove. His deep-set, black and yellow eyes were slightly bloodshot, but there was a hint of kindness behind them.

He looked right at me and as he shook my hand he broke out into a jack-o'-lantern smile. He was only blessed with about half of his teeth; the few left, however, were white and big.

"Ah certain Ah can do all woik ya needs, sir," he began in his high-pitched scratchy voice. One big point for him, no one had ever called me sir before.

"Ah's par-ticular to *po*-lish." - again, like the country - "'Erbert *knows* Ah is a ha'd woika."

He puzzled me, so I made a decision and called my first human resource conference with Herb. I told Speedy Dave to hang on a second while we conferred, and I took Herb outside the office and shut the door behind me.

"You *gotta* be kidding Herb," I said to him. "My sixty-six-year-old grandfather is in better shape than this guy. *Speedy!* You gotta be kiddin' me. It took him a half hour to get out of the car."

Herb had his serious meeting face on. I knew this look; when he was deep in thought his front teeth, largely due to his generous overbite, bit down on his lower lip and he looked a like a rabbit staring at a carrot.

"He maght *be* sixty-six, Chief, don' know that fo' sho'," he said as he tugged on his sparse little beard in thought. "Speed be stronger than he look, though, I seen him run that buffa all day long without no break. He got his name cuz the way he says *sheet*, not cuz how he woik. Takes him maybe thuty minutes ta say it. Once he get woiking though, he don' stop. The 'Erb say he can do it, that oughta be good 'nuff."

"OK, if you think he can do it we'll give him a try. I don't understand, though—he got his nickname because of how he says *shit*?"

"Yassah, you gonna see."

The meeting concluded with Herb giving Dave a sheet of paper with the piecework prices we paid written out on it. Herb took it upon himself to formalize our labor prices, something I had not even thought of. They were written out in a spiral notebook we now kept in the top drawer of the office. His penmanship was perfect; it reminded me of the Palmer writing examples we were taught back in grammar school and I was curious, but had yet to ask, about Herb's education. His spelling was also excellent, and I was, in fact, jealous. Here I was a supposedly well-educated student about to graduate from one of the best private high schools in the state, and my writing was a scrawl compared to Herb's and my spelling was subpar to say the least.

Speed looked at the paper oddly—not sure, I thought, what to make of it.

"This what you gonna get paid," Herb told him. "You add up the jobs an makes a bill fo' the Chief here, ever' Friday. OK, Speed?"

"Tha's fine, 'Erbert," he replied. "If Monday be OK, I see you then. Nace ta meet ya, Mista Steven."

Thus I contracted, other than Herb, whom I now considered a junior partner, the first employee of Reilly Detail.

*****

My cultural indoctrination was beginning to shape up. As it turned out, no one in this new world went by his given name. A nickname or title would be allocated to everyone depending on the varying aspects of their appearance, manner, position, age, etc; titles and nicknames just kind of fell into place. I called Speed "Dave" out of respect for his age, but Herb called him "Speed," as they were longtime friends. Dave thought "Chief" out of place, probably too informal for him, and called me "Mista Steven." I called Herb by his given name but emphasized heavily the *H*, as opposed to his more soothing version, "Eeerb" which

I loved to hear him say. Dave always called him "'Erbert"—again, I thought, out of respect. Herb called me "Chief" when anyone was within earshot, but in our private conversations he called me "boy," a name I grew to detest.

Monday morning, seven a.m. sharp, we all showed up as promised. As I was opening the shop and getting prepared for the day's work, I heard a soon-to-be-familiar phrase coming from my newest employee.

"Who's gonna git the coffee?" Speedy Dave asked me.

"Speed," Herb announced, "cain't woik 'lessun he gets his coffee."

"What do you want *me* to do?" I replied. "We need to get to work."

"Why don' you get down ta Winkel's an git us some coffee," was Herb's solution. "Ah can git Speed set up while you gone."

Time was wasting, so I jumped into my old blue Ford and set out for "Winkel's" (Winchell's Donuts). On my way to the car, Speed shouted out, "Lossa cream, lossa suga', Mista Steven!"

I made my way there and back as fast as my old oil burner would take me. Determined not to make a mistake and have to go back, I brought back three extra-large coffees, equivalent to a good-size pot. In addition to the coffee, they gave me a white paper bag filled with a large container of cream, about twenty-five packages of sugar, and three buttermilk donuts. I laid the feast out on the old maple office desk and called everyone in.

Deferentially, I sat and waited for my employees to prepare their coffee. Herb, with Speed close behind, walked out and dumped about a quarter of his coffee into the defunct planter that fronted the office. They then both proceeded to fill their partially empty cups with cream to just below the rim. Herb opened about five packs of sugar and dumped them all into his brown liquid with Speed following suit in what was to become an agonizingly slow daily ritual. Speed opened each pack of sugar by methodically tearing off the top of each one, emptying the contents into the cup, then throwing away the one empty packet. After emptying all fifteen packets, which seemed, in my impatience, to take about a half an hour, he picked up one of the wooden stirring sticks "Winkel's" provided and began stirring the concoction.

Over time, what had once been black coffee had been turned by Speed into a thick, syrupy goo. I was hoping the ceremony was now nearing its conclusion as none of us had yet to touch a car. Dave lazily threw the wooden stirrer into the trash, turned around, and gazed down at his creation with a look of wonder. Ever so carefully, he gently picked up the cup with both hands and took a sip.

Herb and I were now entranced, wondering what the verdict would be. Was the coffee to his liking? Had I procured the right ingredients? Had he mixed those ingredients properly? Would we ever begin to *work* at some point?

His jaws moved. Gradually they parted, the thin lips spreading out wider and wider. Yes, finally he smiled that big toothless grin of his. Success at last! I felt as if an enormous weight was lifted from my shoulders.

I could now relax, and I took in the scene of the two men sitting with me as we all drank our coffee. It was a special moment, one that transformed, into an experience. I was suddenly *not* in such a hurry for us to get to work.

The two men held their cups tightly, with both hands. It was a natural inclination that kept the coffee warm while simultaneously allowing them to feel the tactile sensation of enjoying a hot beverage. I, the neophyte, held mine in one hand.

We drank our coffee in silence, each one looking down into our cups while occasionally looking up at each other. The smiles we displayed were not big and toothy, they were just knowing, satisfied, grins.

I looked across at Herb's coffee cup that he smothered with his big gnarly hands. The coffee inside was the color of cocoa and almost matched Herb's skin. If he were to spill coffee on his arm, you would never even know it.

Dave's coffee, in contrast, was a thick alabaster, with just a hint of tan to let you know there was any coffee in it at all. His coal black hands that hid the brown Winchell's cup made the liquid seem even lighter than it was.

I used a single lily-white hand to lift my cup, and I took a measured swallow. I drank it black, due to the fact I never drank coffee and wanted to try it unadulterated. It tasted bitter at first, but as I saw my comrades lazily sipping the hot coffee, I did the same, and rolled the warm liquid across my tongue. The sensation was a new, exotic, almost an erotic experience, and it took me to a faraway place; far from that dingy office, far from Fullerton, and far from my childhood.

I set the cup down and looked into the cup. The coffee was black; no, more of a burnt brown, auburn, or hazelnut, with a silver sheen on top that reflected the morning sunlight coming in through the office window. Winchell's made coffee differently, I thought. Every cup I had seen until then looked the same; a dull, flat black.

Then again, maybe it wasn't the coffee that was so intriguing. I was drinking it with two men, my colleagues, and my friends. Herb and Dave had been drinking coffee together for years and it was part of a ritual, part of their culture, part of who they were. Yet here I was, accepted by them, part of the group. They had let me into their exclusive club, accepted me for who I was, and it felt glorious.

I have been a coffee drinker ever since; I drink it black, with two hands. The rich flavor of the coffee bean continues to transport me to those same faraway places. Gazing down into the cup, I search for those rich, complex colors that remind me of that day.

Herb broke the silence, as I never would have.

"Speed," he proclaimed, "he laks his coffee sweet. Tha's what makes him sweet hisself, his coffee. Tha's why he gets so much poosy, 'cause he's so sweet from drinkin' his coffee. Heh heh heh."

I knew then, by the look on Speed's face, that we were on the verge of something very special. I had yet to hear it, but somehow, deep inside, I knew it was at hand. Herb smiled his wide, knowing smile, and looked right at me. He knew it was coming too. The room fell silent once again. Speed looked down and to his right, his smile now more serious, but still apparent. I looked at his perforated teeth, Herb and I now both staring at him in anticipation. There was a quiet, powerful tension in the room, and then it came: a low growl coming from somewhere deep down in Speed's gut that began faintly, and ended with a tremendous crescendo:

"shhhhhhhhhhhhhhHHHHHHEEEEEEEEEEEEIIIIIII
TTTTTTTTTTTTT!!!!"

It was, absolutely, world class. I swear it felt as if twenty minutes had passed while the one word crawled out of his mouth. My own mouth was agape. I had never in my life heard one word strung out like that. It not only had length, it had depth and inflection. Herb looked at me like a proud father. He didn't need to say a word; we both knew this was how "Speed" had been awarded his nickname.

That afternoon I realized I had entered a new world with an extraordinary cast of characters, characters who were not like me, not like anyone I knew. Something told me, however, that although I liked these strange people, this new life of mine, the future would not be as sweet, or as smooth, as Speed's coffee.

Chapter Five

THE DRIVER

O ur group fell into a steady routine. Herb was good at cleaning and painting motors, Speed proved to be an exceptional polish and wax man, and I was, as usual, stuck cleaning those filthy interiors. Herb created an assembly line whereby each car moved through the shop into areas that we designated for a specific purpose: engine painting first, interior second, polish and wax next, then the final inspection.

The work was hard, but we became more efficient over time. I knew we were making money when I heard the loud whine of Speed's polishing machine, the air compressor chugging out pressure for Herb's paint sprayer, or the whining of my heavy-duty wet/dry vacuum cleaner.

Through the constant din of our work there was always the sound of music playing in the background, great music, as I was to learn. Speed liked jazz; Herb preferred the blues; I loved the old rock 'n' roll greats my older sister had listened to when I was just a kid. Speed had a beat-up AM/FM radio that he turned on first thing in the morning and it played all day until the last job finished up. Often, when the two men were lost in their work, one or both would sing along with Billie Holiday, Howlin' Wolf, or Muddy Waters, while I couldn't wait for a Fats Domino or Chuck Berry song to play on some staticky FM station Speed knew about.

Our ultimate success, however, was tied to the cost of delivery. It was the responsibility of the detail shop to both pick up automobiles from the customers and deliver them back when they were finished. The Chevrolet dealership my father worked at was approximately fifteen miles east of the shop in an even smoggier suburb of Los Angeles called Whittier. It was best known for the college Richard Nixon had attended, but I knew it only as a long and difficult drive. None of the famous Southern California freeways found their way directly there, so it took about thirty-five minutes each way to deliver a car. This meant that an hour per car, per day, might be wasted on driving.

In a search for efficiency, I appointed myself the primary driver. I knew the short cuts, and I was young and crazy enough to drive silly fast. No one had ever beaten my time to or from Doug Schultz Chevrolet. The secondary reason was that my employees were much better at detailing than me. Herb and Speed were real professionals: I was always amazed at what they'd accomplished by the end of each day.

As business picked up, and the need to deliver more cars reached critical mass, I was forced to create a new position: I needed a part-time driver.

At around three o'clock on a busy Friday afternoon, Speed flipped off his buffer and called out "They is somebody lookin' round onna lot, Mista Steven."

I switched off my vacuum cleaner. I could see him now; it was Jack.

Jack was my best, and only, friend. He too attended St. James, and he, like me, was an outcast, perhaps even more so. He also came from a poor family like mine that preferred to send their kids to Catholic school rather than pay the rent. This forced him to be, like me, an entrepreneurial teenager, and he juggled two jobs while always looking for another. His workload left him outside the mainstream of the St. James High School social world, which was neatly divided into very specific groups.

There were the *Jocks*: Football, basketball, and baseball athletes only. Those in track and field, golf, and swimming, of course, were not permitted into this group.

Next were the *Geeks*: These were academically superior students, who even had their own class, called Honors.

The other two groups were much admired. The barriers to entry: significant.

Surfers: These were self-described, that's what they did after school and in the summertime. They spoke a unique language all of their own: *hodad, gremmie, hang ten, kaak, wipe out, greaser*, and many other pearls of distinct verbiage that grew out of the uniquely Southern Californian surf culture.

Cool Dudes: These *ubermensch* stood head and shoulders above every other group. They were so cool in their look, speech, and charisma as to have ultimate power over every other group.

Jack and I belonged to none of these groups. Not only did we have a healthy independent streak and preferred not to group up, we worked, and had very little time for outside activities.

My friend, Jack Brown, was a lost soul wandering through the social wilderness of the 1960s. A former surfer, and now a musician, he was transitioning into what would later be known as a "hippie," and kind of stuck in between the three worlds. Southern California was holding on tight to its surfer music and clean-cut image a la Annette Funicello and *Beach Blanket Bingo*. The British Invasion, however, was slowly dragging everyone into a drug-and-free-sex-crazy culture that was hard for all of us at St. James to grasp. Jack understood it all, saw it all coming, and was gradually morphing into the give-peace-a-chance generation. He just wasn't quite there yet.

He worked at a fast-food restaurant part-time but at nights played the drums in a surf band that was also trying to adapt to the changing times. It featured a lead singer with a deep voice who could fake a British accent and loved the Beatles and the Rolling Stones. The problem with the group was that the venues they played in Southern California demanded surf music. The band tried to combine the two, and it often sounded like Mick Jagger singing "Surfin' USA" by the Beach Boys, with Jack singing the high parts in the background. Jack's voice had never really changed, and it always sounded like a nervous falsetto a la Barney Fife on *The Andy Griffith Show*.

Herb also spotted Jack out on the lot and decided to run interference for me. He dropped his paint gun and approached what had to be, to him, anyway, a very strange-looking human being. Jack had a flat, freckled face, was several inches shorter than me, and even slighter of build. He had just left Clown Burger, his main source of employment, and still had his uniform on. He must have loved that uniform as he wore it wherever he went. I thought perhaps it identified him as a member of a group, when no other group would have him.

He wore dark blue uniform pants, loose fitting, with an extra-long plain black belt cinching up his waistband. His white shirt and paper sailor's hat were very official looking and required of all Clown employees. Over his breast pocket and on the right side of his hat were the brightly embossed Clown Burger logos.

I knew the uniform didn't strike Herb as unusual; it was the hair. Hairstyles at that time were crucial in defining both social status and class identification.

Jocks had a "number 00" or "number 0" haircut, which meant that their heads were almost clean-shaven.

Geeks had about an eighth of an inch of hair evenly disbursed over the head.

Surfers had around a quarter inch, well kempt, but with a nice long shock of hair above the forehead. When in school, they would comb the sun, or peroxide, bleached hair straight back, but at the beach it had to fall across the forehead, hopefully just touching the eyes.

Cool Dudes were very much like surfers, they preferred it a bit shorter in front, and it was unnecessary to bleach the hair.

I leaned toward the surfer haircut, with just a hint of cool dude. My hair was light brown, conservatively cut, with a slight longish shock of hair in the front, always parted to one side.

Jack, on the other hand, was as confused tonsorially as he was psychologically. Because he played in a band and needed the money, our dean of discipline, Father Ryan, gave Jack special permission to defy the St. James haircut rule. The rule required that no hair touch the ear, and no hair could touch the back of the collar. Father Ryan allowed Jack an exception to one part of the rule, but not to both. Jack chose to have it long and shaggy on both sides, short in the front and short in the back. It looked like a Beatles haircut run over with a lawn mower and with his hat on he appeared to mimic the clown embossed on his shirt.

"Dude, looking for Stevie," he said in his nervous alto voice to the strange black man standing in front of him.

Herb couldn't take his eyes off of him.

"Hey, Chief," he called out, "some—thin's out here lookin' for ya."

I walked out and noticed that Herb remained transfixed by my friend in a very quizzical, yet nonthreatening manner. Jack reciprocated the look. Jack was as sheltered as I was, and had never met an African American man face-to-face, especially one covered with paint and polish from head to toe.

I walked over and began the introductions;

"Herb, this is my friend Jack from school, he's gonna help us deliver cars in the afternoon."

I assumed they both might be gentlemen enough to shake hands, but they did not. They stood transfixed.

Jack broke the silence.

"Dude," was all he said.

"I ain't no *dude*," Herb called out, "and ah don' know no *dude, boy.* You *is* a boy? *Ain't* you?"

Herb turned and asked me, "He a boy, Chief?"

"Yeah, he's a boy," I replied. "He wears his hair like that because he plays in a band. It looks worse with that hat on, but he *is* a boy."

Herb's comment did not faze Jack; he had heard it before.

"Wazzat on your hat, boy?" Herb asked him. "Look like you, little bit, 'cept-in it got or-ange hair."

"That's the clown, Herb," I said to him. "Jack works at Clown Burger."

"Wazzat in his mouth? It look like he be puking up somethin'."

"That's a burger," I answered. "The clown's got a hamburger in his mouth."

A look of comprehension came over Herb's face and he smiled.

"Yaaas, I know the place, they got the bes' fried pies. Ah do *love* them fried pies."

Jack looked to me for help.

"Those apple turnovers you put in the French fry fat," I told him. "We get those with coffee sometimes in the morning. The guys love 'em."

Jack broke out with his own smile in recognition.

"I gotcha now, man," Jack told him. "Those things are dopey good, far out, man."

"Look, Herb," I said, "we need to pick up a couple of cars at Doug Schultz and take this Volkswagen back. Jack's going with us, he's our new driver."

Herb looked dubious, probably about Jack's ability to drive, or it could have been his limited communication skills, I wasn't sure which. The three of us hopped into a 1965 Volkswagen Beetle and took off.

Chapter Six

COLLOQUIALISMS

I drove; I always drove, I was fast. Herb took advantage of his company seniority to ride shotgun and Jack, the new guy, was in back. As I focused on my driving skills so we could make it up to Whittier in record time, Herb turned his attention to Jack.

"The chief heah," he began, "say you playin' in a band, boy. You playin' Muddy Wattas in that band?"

"Man, I don't know that song, dude," he replied. "We play trippy stuff, you know, Animals and Stones, Boys of the Beach, '*Baby Please Don't Go*.' It's groovy, surf, rock shit, man."

Herb looked at me.

"They play rock 'n' roll," I told him. "You know, like the Rolling Stones and Beach Boys."

"Ah don' know no boys at no beach," he replied, "but Ah heard of them Rollin' Ova Stones boys. Boy, don't you know nuthin' bout music?" he said to Jack. "Them Rollin' boys plays Muddy Wattas, Howlin' Wolf, Johnny Lee Hooka. They *stole* that fane mu-sick an jus' put a fasta beat to it. I got nuthin' 'gainst that. Muddy, he plays with them boys once in Chee-cago. You play mu-sick, you best know yo' mu-sick *his-to-ry*. 'Baby Pul-eze Don't Go' is Muddy Wattas; they done stole it from him."

I glanced in the mirror. Jack had no idea what Herb was saying. It wasn't the content; Jack simply couldn't relate to the cadence or the accent. He had never met anyone like this outside of his little world, let alone the Herb.

"That's bitchin' man." Jack called out to him. "If I only knew what you said man, it would be *really* bitchin'."

"Who's the bitch?" Herb quizzed Jack as he looked into the mirror at him. "He callin' me a bitch? That mop a hair be *my* bitch he get uppity with me."

"No, no," I brokered, "*bitchin'* is a word we use. It means good, great, cool. Jack was sayin' he thought what you said was interesting."

"How he know it interestin' if'n he don' know what Ah said?" Herb astutely remarked.

I saw things clearly then: there was a *major* cultural war going on here, and I was to be the reluctant referee.

I tried to explain: "He said, Jack, that there are blues singers named Muddy Waters and Howlin' Wolf and John Lee Hooker that sang and wrote the music that the Rolling Stones and the Animals play. These groups loved old blues music, so that's what they started singing. The original blues musicians wrote most of the songs you now find on those albums. Herb likes the original artists better."

"Man," Jack replied, "I *did* not *comprehendo!* That is pounding great info man. Wait till I dispense said info with the dudes in my *ensemble*, they are gonna flip out. Hey, you two dudes, we gonna hang ten at trestle's Saturday, then beat a gig at the Bear that night. You dudes should par-ti-ci-pate."

I turned to Herb, who now seemed as frustrated with Jack's speech as a tourist getting directions in Slovakia.

I again interpreted: "He's gonna tell the other band members about Muddy and the boys, Herb. He thinks that's great. The members of the band are going surfing down in San Onofre Saturday, then they are playing at a club in Huntington Beach that night called the Golden Bear. We're invited to go."

Herb leaned over to me and whispered, "Why don' he jus' say that?"

I looked at Herb and ignored Jack. "He just talks like that. Hey, he can't understand you either."

"Wha nat? Ah speak *poifect* anglish. You unnerstan' me fane."

"Yes, but we work with each other every day," I replied. "Look, lots of times you don't understand me either, we just have different accents."

"Yeah," he responded, "but that boy don't speak no anglish. Ah don' know where he from, but he sho ain't from roun' heah."

"You'll get used to it," I said. "Give him a chance."

Herb looked down and thought about it for a minute. He gave it another try by changing the topic.

"You boys gettin' you some good poosy?"

A silent pause hung in the air of the small German car. To Herb, it was just a passing comment, but to me, it was a difficult subject that I just couldn't answer. I reflected on how I was still fatally shy, and so socially awkward that there was no hope of me securing a girlfriend anytime in the near future. Jack had no idea what the question was all about.

"What man?" Jack asked. "What you call me?"

"Poosy," Herb repeated, "wha's about poosy?"

"I ain't no poosy, man."

"That's not what he's sayin', Jack," I jumped in.

"Don' you know wha's poosy boy?" Herb asked him.

"Sure I do, that's what the football players call me. I ain't no pussy and you got no reason to call me that. You ain't keen to my locks don't mean you can throw names down on me man."

Herb looked perplexed. He thought he had offended Jack, but he wasn't sure of how or why.

"Come on, Jack," I tried again to explain, "haven't you ever heard of the slang, crude word for women? *Pussy.* That's why the football players call you that. It's a women's *vagina*, they're calling you a c-u-n-t."

"Oh, yeah, I knew that," Jack said. "I just no *comprendo*, how am I supposed to 'get' a pussy?"

"Herb," I barked at him, "is asking you if you have a girlfriend, you idiot. Are you having any sex?"

"Man, *why* don't he just spit that out?" Jack lashed out. "What is with this crazy dude? Is he from another *planet*, man?"

I ignored his question and attempted to move this strange conversation forward.

"No Herb," I said. "I for one don't have a girlfriend. There are a few girls I would like to get to know, but it's not in the cards for me right now."

"I'm having lots of sex, man," Jack added. "Just be nice to have it with a girl instead of one-on-one, if ya know what I mean. I got a girl, but she's just like, a friend right now. She works night shift at the Clown. I like her tits. Her nipples stick out right where the clown face is on her shirt, they make the clown look like he's spittin' the burger right out of his mouth man."

Herb leaned over to me; "Tha's the onliest thang he done said I unnerstan'."

"Were makin' progress, gentlemen!" I pronounced.

"Somethin' wrong with you boys?" Herb demanded. "You ain't gone sweet on ol' 'Erb, now is ya? Ain't no boys you age, with you looks," - he looked at me with that comment and smiled, he looked back at Jack and just shook his head- "that ought not to has poosy. Ain't right, wazz wrong with you boys?"

"No Herb, we aren't 'sweet,'" I replied. "Think about it. All we do is go to school and work in the winter and in the summer all we do is work. We don't have time for girls."

"Ah don' be-lieves it! You boys got plenty a nights you can getcha some poosy. Somethin' wrong! Ain't raght! Maybe the 'Erb can help you boys out. A man need help with poosy he comes to the 'Erb. 'Erb, he *know* poosy. 'Erb get so much poosy he carry a baseball bat in the car, he got to beat them women back. Now Ah *know* you boys ain't got good looks lak the 'Erb, an' Ah *know* you ain't got the *charrrm* of the 'Erb, but *sointinly* you boys can get leastwise some ugly-ass poosy! Ain't right!"

"You don't understand Herb. Jack and I are outsiders; we don't belong to a group. We aren't football players or rich surfer kids. That's what the girls want. Someday we'll both have lots of time and money and we can get any girl we want. Right now we won't get any girls unless the good Lord blesses our young asses with a miracle."

"With that attitude you ain't. Ah see what you mean. You don' *think* you can get no poosy, so you don' try. That sound lak a *fane* plan to me, boy."

I couldn't come up with a good response; there was a lot of truth in what Herb said. Jack looked despondent; I think I had been a little too blunt in my assessment of our situation for his tender ego. He entered into a silent funk as I shifted into low and turned into the driveway of Doug Schultz Chevrolet.

Chapter Seven

DOUG SCHULTZ CHEVROLET

Doug Schultz was a third-generation family-owned Chevrolet dealership fronting a busy six-lane highway named Whittier Boulevard. Famous for car cruising of the local hamburger joints on Saturday nights, it was a major artery that connected the smog-choked southeastern suburbs of Los Angeles with Orange County just to the south. The used car division of Doug Schultz, which my father oversaw, was a few miles north of the main showroom and operated as an independent operation. The dealership was on a long narrow strip of land that backed up to a hillside, behind which an elevated 1940s housing development lay. Three lengthy rows of perfectly aligned cars faced the highway, backed by a string of smallish offices elevated just above the display area.

As we drove our freshly cleaned VW beetle up onto the main driveway, we were transported into the world of American small business ingenuity and free enterprise. My father embodied this spirit through a combination of his strict Marine Corps discipline and the marketing savvy handed down to him by my grandfather.

Every car on display was spotless, having been wiped down each morning by the "lot boy" whose responsibility it was to clean, start, and align every car daily. All cars displayed a brightly colored plastic sock that slipped over the antenna mast, allowing the attached colored plastic flags to flow eagerly in the dirty wind. An informational decal or lettering was affixed to every windshield. "AIR COND," "LIKE NEW" "GUARANTEED," "100% FINANCE." They all told a brief story people could understand in ten seconds as they whizzed by in their potential trade-in vehicles.

Benjamin Reilly never really wanted to leave the Marine Corps; it left *him* after the war. His office was the first one on the right as you drove in. It was larger than the other offices and had a better view of the cars on display. I always felt he was more comfortable here in his automotive kingdom than he was at home. Here he was in charge and had control over his surroundings. It was *his* used car lot, *his* domain, and *his* regimental office. The man had gone broke, twice, when he owned his own car dealerships before now becoming a used car manager. It had to be a crushing blow for a man who'd risen to captain during the war in the Pacific and who'd operated what was, for a short while, a very successful business afterward. He had lost everything, and now ran a secondhand car business for someone else.

We pulled into the designated guest parking spot in front of his office and prepared for "the inspection." I told Jack to stay outside with Herb as I climbed the steps to his ivory tower. I knocked on the door and then patiently waited for a response.

"Enter," was my greeting from inside the office. I opened the door and presented myself. He sat behind a gray metallic desk looking at paperwork of some sort that appeared to be more important than my presence as he failed to acknowledge anyone had entered the room.

I shared none of his physical characteristics; I clearly took after my mother. He was shorter than I, and where I was lanky, he was rather stocky. Muscular still through his chest and shoulders, he had the look and bearing of a powerful man. His hair was thinning, but still inky black, with a seamless part on the upper left side of his pate revealing a Brylcreem comb-over that failed to cover up his ever-growing forehead. He was, I am now sure, somewhat handsome, although at the time I never saw him as such.

He had on a perfectly tailored brown suit, a crisp white shirt, and a big wide tie embellished by the perfect Windsor knot. He owned several suits like this, all remnants of a time when money was plentiful. Proud of the way he looked, he rotated his suits and ties methodically to keep them in prime condition. He knew he could never buy one again.

I stood up straight and would have looked him right in the eye, but he was preoccupied. I dared to glance around his office. On the front left corner of the old desk was his pipe collection. I don't know where he picked up the habit, but I always assumed high-ranking officers in the military had smoked pipes when he was in the service and it was common to see Pop looking very distinguished with one of his carved wooden pipes falling out of the corner of his mouth.

Sales award plaques of every type wallpapered the rear wall from floor to ceiling and in the far corner was a small table upon which lay his most prized possession: a picture of Benjamin Reilly throwing mock punches at the famous prizefighter Max Baer. It was the highlight of his career, the grand opening of Reilly Motors, long ago forgotten in the dustbin of shuttered used car lots, but still a fond memory for my father.

"We have the '65 beetle sir," I stated bluntly. My father tolerated neither warm greetings nor signs of affection, and under no circumstances were we allowed to call him by a familial name. My brother and I called him Pop to ourselves, but sir was his only name of choice.

"Let's take a look," he replied, as he lifted stiffly out of his chair.

Herb had been through this drill before. He stood next to the freshly cleaned VW at full attention and did a reasonably good job of placing Jack, eyes upright, next to him.

The routine began. My father inspected the car from stem to stern, walking all the way around it, looking underneath it, and then pausing as he looked up at me. I knew the cue well: I popped open the trunk and hood, then lifted the lids. I stepped squarely backward to allow the inspection to continue. He peered into what seemed like every crevice of the car and then turned to what was now a neat row of Reilly Detail employees to make his pronouncement before he noticed the scraggly-headed fellow on the end.

"Jack? What are you doing here?" he called out.

"I'm workin', sir," was his answer. Jack had met my father a few times in the past; he understood well the proper salutation.

"Jack is going to help out delivering cars in the afternoon, sir," I put in. "We're getting pretty busy now with the additional Volkswagen dealer business."

"I see. Is the additional business creating such a strain on your company that your quality has suffered? Who inspected this car before delivery?"

Now we all, except Jack, knew who had inspected the car. It was Herb's job to do a final inspection and my father knew this well.

"Ah did, suh!" Herb declared. "Is somethin' wrong, suh?"

"Are you blind, mister?" replied the captain. "Look at the wax on the rocker panel down here! There's dirt underneath the spare tire! Someone *failed* to remove the spare tire before cleaning the trunk!"

Herb pulled a rag out of his pocket and immediately addressed the various offences.

"Suh, it's ma fault," he began. "Ah take ree-sponsibility. Ah think the car was in the shade an I jes done missed it. Ah promise to be mo' careful. Ah wont you to be com-pull-etely happy with our woik."

"Look," Pop replied, "I can have anyone do my work. There's a place right down the street. You boys either do the job right, or I send it somewhere else." He looked me right in the eye. "If this man can't inspect a car, get someone else. I only have two cars for you now, the blue Impala and that gray truck over there, keys are in them."

With that he made a smart turn for his return to headquarters. Suddenly he snapped his head back toward us as if he had just forgotten something and called out, "Jack."

"Yes sir," Jack replied.

"Get a haircut," he said, walking away.

Herb looked at me and shrugged. He had been through the same drill several times before and he was now used to it. I, however, was not.

"There is no reason for him to treat you like that," I raged at Herb. "Why do you kowtow to him the way you do?"

"Look, boy, we done talked about that. He the boss. He got the powa an' is his cars. He jes a tough biz-ness-man. We the ones got to make him happy, tha's *our* biz-ness. You take it pers-nal. It ain't; jes biz-ness."

I was still angry, angry at my father for yelling at Herb, angry at him for him going broke, angrier even more because I knew we could never be close. I gave Jack the Impala, Herb climbed into the truck with me for the drive home.

Chapter Eight

FATHERS

The old truck was noisy, but in the cab there was a lingering silence. I was still annoyed when Herb remarked, "He still you daddy, you know. You lucky to have a daddy, some boys neva has one."

I wasn't sure if he was looking for a reply, but there was something unsettled in me. I could taste it. It was sour, deep, and stubborn. I taste it still.

"I don't *feel* like I even *have* a father," I finally replied. "I never see him at home. He works all the time or is out at night drowning his sorrows in a bar somewhere. When I do see him, he gives me a command like I was one of his soldiers. I give him a yes sir or a no sir and that's the end of our conversation. I have to *pay rent* to live at home and he couldn't care less where I am or how I'm doing in school. I'm not complaining, Herb, I get to come and go as I please, sometimes I just wonder what other fathers are like."

"Sound's from what Ah heard he had a run a bad luck, son. You got to forgive a man that been through ha'd tames. Man that been up, when he go down, he go down ha'd. He jes wants the best fo' his fam'ly, now he feels low, cain't give 'em what he wonts."

"It has nothing to do with his lack of success. I had to grow up with him, you didn't. He's one tough old bird that doesn't give a shit about his kids, that's it, that's all there is to it."

There was a chill inside the old truck. It had no heater, but then again, it wouldn't have mattered. Herb looked straight ahead; his face was shrouded in sadness.

I never took note of, or cared for, emotions or feelings. I was an impassive teenager living in a callous home. Like most teenagers, I was selfish, and not a little narcissistic. There was no girlfriend in my life, and my only friend seemed as disconnected from his family as I was from mine. Sitting next to Herb now, I sensed something different. I saw sorrow in his face, and I cared. He was troubled, and I felt a deep sympathy for him. My sympathy then mutated, into *empathy*, as I genuinely *felt* his sorrow. This was a new feeling for me, and it did not come naturally; I had learned from example that people needed to take care of their *own* selves, both physically and emotionally.

I wanted to find out what Herb was thinking, but was not sure how to broach the subject.

"What about *your* father?" I mumbled. "What's he like?"

"He's daid. He dayed in a fiya in Chee-cago 'bout ten years ago."

"Sheeiiit"—I had become very proud of the way I could draw the word out by then— "that's too bad. What was he like?"

"Oh, he a great man. He were a good husban' and he love his fam'ly. He fought in the wah, fust wah, got a special letta from Gen'ral Perching. Was a hero, he was, yas, he were a *great* man."

"Was he good to you? Were you two close?"

"Don' rightly know 'bout that. Neva met him."

"Really? Then how do you know about him?"

Herb shuffled his feet and looked out the side window at nothing in particular.

"Momma tol' me. She tol' me 'bout his bein' a hero in the wah and she tol' me he was a good man to her. He went to find woik. We needed money so's he went off looking for woik an' we never seen him ag'in. Mama said if'n he foun' a job he would send fer us, but he neva did. Tames got real tough back in Lou's'ana an' we took off ta fand him. We foun' him in Chee-cago, but he was daid."

"Wow, you grew up without a dad, that had to be tough. At least I had a dad."

"I had me a daddy, boy!" he reprimanded me. "I had me a *good* daddy, he jes wadn't able to be with us, he was lookin' for woik. He love my momma, and he love me, boy."

There was pain and anger in his voice. I sensed it wasn't necessarily directed at me, but I was on untested ground, and knew to proceed with caution.

"I'm sure he would have been a great father to you," I fumbled out. "He wouldn't have been at all like my dad."

"Boy, I don' wanna *eva* heah you com-plain 'bout yo' daddy no mo'! You got nothin' to com-plain 'bout. You livin' in a nice house, you eatin' good food, you goin' to a high fa-lut-in school. Sheeet, you pro'ly goin' to some fancy college someday. You got more 'vantages than anabody I know. I don' wanna hear 'bout you payin' rent, or you has to woik so ha'd. *Ever'body* has to woik ha'd. *Lafe* is ha'd, sooner you face that, sooner you gonna be a *grown* man."

The comment slid under my delicate skin and I wanted to lash out at him. I held back for a moment as I was angry, partly because he sounded a little like my father, and partly because he was right. I looked at his face; it had changed dramatically. A knowing look of self-righteousness now encompassed him and it occurred to me that someone, Herb, might actually care about my welfare, and about me. My anger melted away and my mind wandered to the *tone* of the conversation. I was participating in a *genuine* conversation with another human being, intelligent conversation, ripe with information, honesty, and emotion. It was a new experience, a new skill, it felt good, and I craved more.

"Herb, how old were you when you left Louisiana?" I asked him. "Did you go to school in Chicago? What was that like?"

"Moved from Lou's'ana when Ah was 'bout ten. We run outta money when Ah was in ha school. Grade ten Ah think it was. Mama was cleanin' houses, daddy was daid, an Ah had to go ta woik, so's Ah got me a job cleanin' cars. Been doin' that eva since."

"What if you didn't have to go to work? Would you have stayed in school? Did you like school?"

I was curious. I knew Herb was intelligent: I always admired his beautiful handwriting on the invoices and notes he wrote, and his spelling was flawless. I had a hard time putting his writing together with the way he spoke.

"Yassa, I did love my schoolin'," he reminisced. "Ma teacha said I was the best student in the class. She had hopes fo' me, sure. Said I was college mat-er-ial. Ah was good in 'rithmatic and I could write me a *fane* story. I read me lots a books, many as you, Ah bet."

There was a wistful look in his eyes. I knew I was treading on ever more sensitive ground.

"Your handwriting is really good, much better than mine," I remarked. "Did someone teach you proper English and grammar at that school?"

I knew at once that I had phrased the remark improperly. He squinted, and began to speak methodically, clearly pronouncing every word.

"Son, Ah can speak an-glish as good as you. Ma teacher was an educated woman. She believed no matter what, Ah should speak and write good an-glish. Ah can speak and write as well as any man, that includes you, boy."

It stunned me. His rhetoric was clear and concise although accented.

"Why don't you speak like that all the time, Herb? Your teacher would be proud of you. You could really impress people if you spoke like that."

"That ain't who I *am*, boy. Ah ain't tryin' to impress *nobody*. Ah'm a Lou's'ana boy, an' tha's how we talk in Lou's'ana. Ma frens talk lak me, ma fam'ly talk lak me, an Ah don' need to be someone Ah ain't. Teacha was a fine woman, but she was wrong 'bout that. You don' make fun no one speaks diff'rent from you, boy, eva. You don' know what they lak inside from lookin' at the outside. You gots'ta get way deep inside ta see what a man all about. Unnerstan', boy?"

"Yeah, I unnerstan'. *You* have to understand, though, I've never been around anyone like you or Speed, and I'm still trying to figure that inside-and-outside thing out."

45

"'At's OK, boy. Some men looking down at other men cause they look diff'rent or they speak diff'rent. Ah know you a good boy, Ah jes wont to make sure you allas listen to the 'Erb when it comes to treatin' folks with respect. That includes yo' frens an yo' fam'ly; yo' daddy too."

My father was the tough one, I had to think about that, but we both knew some significant advice had passed between us.

I shifted the old truck into low as we pulled up into the driveway of the rusty old gas station where we worked. It looked the same, yet everything seemed so different.

Chapter Nine

LANCE-A-LOT

There was plenty of work for us, but it sometimes came in cycles. Some days we were busy, and some not so much. Herb whistled his way into my office one morning late in August of that year and made an announcement.

"We needs mo' woik. If we had us a few mo' car dealas we could make the woik mo' steady. Ah heard from my fren "Cheata"—a married but faithless gentleman who worked at Gussie's—"that Lance-A-Lot lookin' fo' a new shop. Lance a good fella, sells lotsa cars. I think we got to go see him this aftanoon, Chief."

So off we drove together in a blue 1960 Oldsmobile 98 that wanted to go back home to Doug Shultz that afternoon. I guided the gigantic automobile down Commonwealth Boulevard until we hit the Lance-A-Lot caratorium just a few miles from Reilly Detail.

I had seen the place before; you could hardly miss it. The large, hand-painted, wooden sign over the little white office summed it all up:

LANCE-A-LOT
Fine Imported Automobiles

It was, like so many others, a classic used car lot carved out of the downtown business district during the car-starved post–World War Two era. There were five sagging rows of clear electric light bulbs

47

hanging across the length of the entire lot. In between the strings of lights were rows of brightly colored red-white-and-blue banners that beckoned to anyone in quest of a good deal on a used car. A small, plain, white wooden office sat in the center of the lot about three-quarters of the way back. As we approached, the door swung wide open and out popped what I assumed to be the proprietor of the establishment, Lance Chesworth.

He was short and a bit portly. His mostly bald head was partially covered with a massive comb-over that started just about a quarter inch above his right ear and reached completely over his pate, almost touching the opposite ear. The dye in his hair was intended to be a youthful reddish brown but through some unfortunate set of circumstances it had turned his hair a distinct shade of burnt orange crowned by a ring of gray that began at his longish sideburns and continued on around the back of his neck.

His nose was ruddy and dark red, a condition shared by many of the auto salesmen I met back then. He wore a thick plaid wool jacket accented by a bright red ascot that seemed out of place considering it was the middle of summer and about ninety-five degrees out. His pants were wool, dark blue, and highlighted by a white belt and matching white patent leather shoes.

F. Scott Fitzgerald glasses framed his ruddy face; the perfectly round lenses were secured by what seemed to be very expensive tortoiseshell frames. Very cool, I thought, very European.

He attacked us with wide-open arms and a million-dollar smile.

"Well well, *Herbert*, my good man, so jolly good to see you," he said with a very warm British accent. "And is this the young bloke you spoke to me about? *Hello*, young man, may I assume you are Herbert's protégé?" he said as he proffered his puffy white hand to me.

"Lance, this here's Steven. Steven, this here's Lance, Lance, ah, ah, Ches-wooly."

"Chesworth, son," Lance corrected him. "You may call me Lance if you wish, we certainly don't go on convention here. Welcome to my marketplace of automotive delicacies, my boy. Here at Lance-A-Lot I solicit only the finest late-model carriages of European lineage."

He raised his arm and waved it across the seedy lot.

"Look around you, my boy! Feast your eyes on the finest artwork the Continent has ever produced."

I did as I was instructed to do. I slowly gazed from side to side, taking in one by one some of the cars I had only dreamed about. Yes, dreamed; most teenagers dream about their anxieties, or in the case of boys, sex; I dreamed about cars. The white 1963 MGB over to my right: dreamed about it. The red 1962 Alfa Romeo Giulietta on the front row: dreamed about it. The 1960 yellow bathtub Porsche right behind us: dreamed about that *many* times.

Sometimes I was alone; sometimes I had a girl in the car. Sometimes, I would leave home on a long trip with Jack in a Chevrolet Corvette like the guys in the TV series *Route 66*. One night I even dreamed I was driving down Pacific Coast Highway in a 1955 Porsche 550 Spyder watching the waves roll in like James Dean would have done. I didn't know for sure, but I thought the dreams might be traced to the fact that I had logged more miles in a car since I had earned my driver's license than just about any other teenager on the face of the earth. I did know, however, that I loved driving, and I loved cars.

Herb shattered my dreams by getting right to the point.

"Lance, we hear you need a good detail shop. What you think about us doing yo' cars?"

"Well, my good man," he responded, "what is your tariff to tidy up one of these fine vehicles? Keep in mind, now, they are a wee bit slighter in size than those monstrous American machines you are used to dealing with."

"Twen'y-two fifty," Herb barked out.

"Twenty-two fifty!" Lance chirped back. "My good man, Gussie charges only twenty American dollars. Why, that, I believe, is highway robbery! Certainly can't let that happen, now can we?"

Herb then turned to face Lance directly and changed his tone.

"You and Ah *know* Gussie jes lose her crew fer peddlin' sex favahs all ova town. You need a de-*pendable* shop do yo' woik. We the best shop in town, we do quality woik, and we don't do no sex favahs, so get that straight."

Our main competition, Gussie, had a very unique, and for a time, successful business model. She hired mostly women, some of ill repute, to do her work. In order to increase business Gussie would send a worker up to do an occasional sexual favor for the dealer's used car manager. Apparently some of Gussie's workers had gotten a little greedy, someone got mad, and the local police were called in. The cops set up a sting at Fullerton Ford one Friday night and they took most of Gussie's crew, three salesmen, and the used car manager into custody. Gussie's legal issues gave us our big chance to fill the vacuum left behind.

Lance was obviously irritated at Herb's suggestion that he would deal with such a shady organization as Gussie's. He slid his expensive glasses off in disgust and cleaned each lens carefully with the silk handkerchief that peeked out of his breast pocket. It was about then that I noticed the lenses were perfectly clear.

"Herb, let's knock off fifty cents," I said. "His cars are a bit smaller, although those wire wheels *are* a pain in the ass to clean."

"Well, the youth speaks," Lance remarked. "I will agree, but only on a trial basis. Twenty-two dollars for first-class workmanship. I am able to proffer you approximately two cars per day on average. Do we have a deal, my good men?"

Herb piped up first. "We got a deal."

Lance then cocked his head and looked at me.

"And what fine automobile are *you* currently driving, my boy?"

"I've got a '54 Ford, it ain't much to look at, but it's dependable," I told him.

"Can I show you something, Steven?" he whispered in my ear.

"Sure." I shrugged.

My curiosity led me to follow him around the back of the little office and, sitting there, hidden from view, was a 1963 Sunbeam Alpine. The smallish sports car was made by Sunbeam, a British company, which, after going broke, had been acquired by Rootes, another British company that would also go broke. They were subsequently acquired by Chrysler, an American company that was also destined to go broke.

The car had been built to compete with the MGs and Triumph sports cars of the era, but it never really took off. Not a bad-looking car, it was a rather plain two-seat sports model with a convertible top.

This one was a beauty. British racing green with a black interior, it had wire wheels and a black top that was now lowered to reveal its best attributes.

I knew the car well. My father was a Sunbeam dealer and had sold a few of these mechanically delicate automobiles for a short time before he too went broke. It had a 1,759 cc four-cylinder engine and was, as were most British cars, greatly underpowered.

"My boy," Lance began, "I just took this exceptional automobile in trade. It is a fine steed indeed, a proper ride for a young man out and about such as yourself. No offense, but a man of your industriousness and good looks should not be driving a 1954 Ford." Then he said slyly in my ear, "Would you happen to be a ladies' man, Steven?"

His elegant pitch swirled around the dark green sportster and I was smitten. I sat behind the wheel and once again soared into automotive dreamland. This time I was driving, fast, much faster than the little piece of shit would go, and I was with a girl, a faceless girl, but *full* figured.

Herb, who had been following the proceedings closely, decided to intervene. "How much you wan' fo' this piece a junk, Lance?"

"Why," he replied, "for your young associate here, I would sell it for what I paid for it, four hundred and fifty US dollars. It might sell for as high as nine hundred dollars on the retail market. I would venture the young man could drive it for a period of time, sell it, and make a tidy profit. Why, if you like, I could deduct the value of your work from the price. A few hundred down and we could easily work out the rest."

I was sold. I wanted to drive it home, pick up Jack, and cruise Bob's Big Boy hamburger stand that very night. Better yet, I wanted my father to see it sitting out in front of the house, a true sign of my newfound success.

"Wha's thet rust on thet brake rotor theah, Lance?" Herb asked. "Those brakes got to be re-placed. Staht the engine, boy."

I turned the key and the ignition sluggishly turned the motor over. After what seemed like forever, the engine finally caught and I gave it a little gas. *Ka-thump-ka-thump ka-thump.* It sounded OK to me; I thought English engines all sounded that way.

"Lance, that car got a bad valve," Herb proclaimed.

"Oh," Lance replied, "perhaps, but you know, any used car might need a tune-up. The boy could spend a few dollars on the car, but it will be well worth the money in the long run."

"Chief." Herb turned to me. "Leastwise you got brakes, valve job, tune-up. It 'pears to me likewise you needs a batt'ry an' a stahta. This car ain't no Chevy. Those parts cost lotsa money. Ah think you gonna spend five hunnert leastwise on this piece a junk jes to git her runnin'. You got that kinda money?"

Crash landing; dreams destroyed, again, by another practical adult. I got out of the old piece of sheeiiit and closed the door.

"I don't think I can afford it right now, Lance," I said. "Let me make some money first and I'll see what you have in a few months."

Lance looked at Herb and just shrugged his shoulders.

"Well, it certainly would have been a wise purchase," he opined.

The excitement of his sales pitch riled me all up and I had to pee.

"Lance, can I use your bathroom?" I asked.

"Certainly, my good man, just go back around the front of the office and you will see the loo inside."

I walked around to the front of Lance's small office and found a narrow door with a handwritten "WC" on it. I went inside and while gratefully relieving myself I heard Herb talking to someone outside through the small vent window in the bathroom that opened to the rear of the office. I quietly unlatched the window and lowered it, the voices now becoming clear and unimpeded.

"I had to try," the first, unfamiliar, voice said.

"Ah know," I heard Herb's voice say.

"Look, he seems like a good kid, you got a good gig goin' over there.

I'll give ya some work, Herbie, jest don' mess it up. Listen, I'm short on cash right now and not lookin' to face the Roach. He's lookin' for me and I know he's a friend of yours. Do me a favor, Herbie, here's a hundred, give it to him and tell him I'll get him the rest next week."

I peeked through the grimy old blinds and saw it was Lance giving Herb a stash of twenty-dollar bills. Herb took it and stuffed it into his back pocket.

"You gotta stay away from them ponies, Larry," Herb replied. "You don't know 'em like the 'Erb does. 'Erb make a bet with the Roach he knows what gonna win. If'n you don't know which ponies gonna win you betta not bet with the Roach. Ah take care of that Roach fer ya this tame, but Ah'm collectin' fo' us from now on, not that bookie Roach. That boy, he's a good boy, Ah like woiking with him an' Speed. We do good woik, Larry, you jes be sho you don' owe the Roach mo' money then you owe me."

"Thanks, Herbie," Lance replied, "but it ain't like that. I ain't playin' the ponies, he loaned me the seed money for the lot here and I ain't ever been able to get caught up. Now look, get your ass outta here, I got a customer comin' in who's a grape, and Lance here needs to squeeze him. Sucker wants to buy that rusty ol' Jag out there."

I had to look again. It *was* Lance; only it was not his voice. There was no accent, no airs, no nothing. I couldn't believe my ears. I quietly shut the window and walked back to the two men standing behind the office.

"Let's go, Herb, we got work to do!" I said.

Lance, or whoever it was, spoke to me.

"Well, my good man, it has been absolutely *maaavelous* meeting you. Come by tomorrow and I will have two vehicles for you to freshen up."

"See you, *Lance*," I said as I turned and walked away.

*****

On the way to Doug Schultz I revealed to Herb what I had overheard.

"You knew the guy was a phony, Herb. Why not let me in on it? I feel like a fool, plus he almost sold me a car."

"Sorry, boy, he been doing that Lance thang a long tame now. He get so he ain't always sure who he is hisself, but he got *prade* an' I figure it fo' *him* to let people know who he is fo' sho. Real name's Cheatly, Larry Cheatly. He ain't a bad man, boy, he jes' a born sale'man. Man takes prade in what he do, he be the one tell you 'bout it, boy, not me. Beside which, it be bad if he sells cars an' go by that name he been stuck with. Un-fo'-tu-nut he got that name. Cain't blame him wantin' to change that."

"What was the hundred dollars for?" I asked him. "And who, or what, is the Roach?"

"A fren, tha's all. Cheat-ly owes him money; tha's all. Don' worry none 'bout the Roach, ain't yo' biz-ness."

That closed the subject, but I knew there was more to learn about this Roach guy, and I probably would.

It took six months before Lance would let down his guard and reveal his true identity to me. He called one afternoon and asked me to pick him up and take him home. He was sitting at the far end of the bar at the Wagon Wheel restaurant, drunk as a skunk. Larry Cheatly, three sheets to the wind, finally came clean.

Chapter Ten

THE CALHOUN'S

My small enterprise was beginning to flourish. The addition of Lance-A-Lot and Lee Adkins Volkswagen, however, was straining my thin labor pool. Herb foresaw the looming crisis and had been telling me we needed more help. I relied on Herb to put the word out around town regarding our new employment opportunities, and sure enough, he came through.

After delivering a car one afternoon, I entered my office and was greeted by the undersides of two large, well-worn work shoes lying on top of my desk. A copy of Herb's latest horse racing paper hid the intruder's face.

"Can I help you?" I asked the faceless visitor.

I startled the stranger; he leaned too far back in my chair and crashed into the wall behind him while simultaneously tossing today's trifecta straight up into the air.

"Whoa, ya sceered me, young fella," he said as he gathered himself back up onto his feet.

"Sorry, mister, what can I do for you?" I asked him.

"Ah'm lookin' fer Mr. Railey, boy, he 'roun'?"

"He doesn't work here," I answered him. "He's the manager at Doug Schultz Chevrolet up in Whittier. You know where that is?"

"Ah was tol' he owns this here detailin' shop. If he up theah, then *who* runs this here detail shop?"

It finally occurred to me that the large white gentleman facing me was looking for the Mr. "Railey" standing in front of him. In my entire life no one had called me "Mr." Reilly except for the good priests at St. James High School.

Assuming a bit of swagger now, I replied to him, "I think I'm the Mr. Reilly you're looking for, Steven Reilly, I own the shop."

"You is Mr. Railey? How old *is* you, boy?"

"Old enough to own this detail shop, mister. Now I need to get back to work, what is it you want?"

He broke out in a big toothy grin and spoke in a most amiable manner.

"Waill Ah'll be, you a young'un to be a boss, thet for sure. Whitey sen' me over. Herb tol' him you need some he'p here an tha's wha Ah'm heah. Name Andrew, boy, Andrew Calhoun. Call me Andy. Come all the way from West 'Ginia jes to clean cars fo' y'all."

He was a big man, about six foot four if you stood him up straight, which you could never do. His potbelly pulled his shoulders down into a distinct slouch resulting in a rounded back, and with his long arms he was somewhat cro-magnon in appearance. He might have been a good-looking man at one time; I guessed him to be about mid-fifties, but like all the men in this business, he was most likely younger than he looked. He had thinning brown hair, deep-set eyes, and a dark farmer's tan. I guessed by the growth on his face that he was a Sunday shaver; it was now Thursday. He offered his smile generously, the main feature being a single gap where one of his eyeteeth should have been. The remaining teeth were stained Marlboro brown, a particular shade I was growing used to seeing by now.

He didn't *have* to tell me what part of the country he was from. I had never met anyone in real life who sounded exactly like Walter Brennan in the TV series *The Real McCoys*, but here he was, the real "Real McCoy", right in front of me.

He wore the now familiar blue work shirt with his name stitched across the top of the pocket. This was, I decided, the sign of a fully qualified detail professional. You didn't have to know how to spell *car* to qualify as a car detailer. You could be a drug addict or a homicidal criminal on the run; it didn't matter. If you showed up with a blue work shirt that had your name embroidered on it, you were fit to be hired on the spot. My own shirt was the right color and texture, but I had yet to figure out the embroidered-name part.

I was nervous, as Herb wasn't there, and I had yet to conduct an employee interview by myself. Unsure of what to do next, I dove into an in-depth and thorough questioning of my applicant worthy of the best HR director at General Motors Corporation. My first probing question was; "When can you start, Andy?"

I knew I should have asked him something, anything, about himself, but my mind went blank.

"Waal, Ah kin be heah tomorra if'n you wont. Do ye wont me ta po-lish"—once more, as in the country— "'n wax?"

"Yea, but I think I need a lot more than that from you. We were doing three to four cars a day and now we will have about six to eight. I usually do some of the work myself, but now I'm going to have to deliver cars most of the time. I really need someone that can do everything."

"Does ya pay piecework?"

"Yes, everything is piecework, it looks like I'll have plenty of work for you to do."

"Then Ah'll bring ma two boys in, we all kin handle whate'r ya got, jes pay me piecework an Ah'll pay the boys. They's good workers, an Ah'll make 'em be heah raght on tame."

This seemed like a reasonable solution to my labor woes. I assumed Andy had, by his age, a couple of grown boys in the business and they would all show up the next day. This could be a blessing as I was looking at six cars out on the lot that needed cleaning and delivery tomorrow.

"See ya tomorry then, pleased ta meet ya, boss," he replied as he shook my hand and slouched off. I wasn't sure what I had just accomplished, but I knew "tomorry" would be interesting.

*****

"Tomorry" came, and I was late to work, as I'd had an early delivery at the Chevy store. I pulled into the shop about ten o'clock and noticed a frenzy of activity taking place. Every car held over from the night before was being worked on. I could not count the number of workers polishing, waxing, cleaning interiors, and painting engines. The usual blues on the radio had been replaced by the sound of blaring fiddles and twanging guitars. I looked for, and spotted, Herb with his head stuck under the hood of a 1958 white Rambler Ambassador station wagon.

"Herb," I yelled over the roar of the machines and the din of the music. "What's going on? Who are all these people?"

"You done hired 'em, Chief," he said. "Andy ova there say you put he an' the fam'ly on las' naght. Good thang you did, boy, we neva git this woik done wit'out 'em. They good woikas, Ah got ta say. Andy woikin' in the back Chief, best go see wha's up, he got half a West 'Ginia woiking in there."

Andy was polishing a 1963 silver Pontiac Bonneville. Quite the luxury car in its time, it took up two full parking spaces inside the garage of the old gas station.

"Howdy, boss," he greeted me. "Good thang we here, lotsa work this mawnin'."

"Andy, who are all these people? I thought it was just you and your two boys?"

"Oh yes indeedy, boss, it was. Than we got heah and foun' all these heah cars needed cleanin'. Ah called up the res' the fam'ly an' got 'em down heah. Don' worry 'bout the money, boss, we all do piecework, stric'ly piecework. If'n we don' need 'em we can send 'em home an' they don' get nuthin'. Let me have ya meet the fam'ly, boss. C'mon with me."

With that, he proceeded to introduce me to all of my new employees.

"This har is my boy Sandy," he began. We stood behind a skinny teenager with an unkempt bush of red hair and a face blotchy with erupting pimples that vied for position with his countless freckles. He was polishing the chrome bumper of a 1964 Ford Galaxie 500. Andy grabbed the unsuspecting boy by the back of his collar, lifted him up, and turned him around in one motion. "This here's the boss, Sandy, say hey to him, boy."

"Hey, boss," he squeaked out. Andy gently let him down and back to work he went. As we turned around, a streak of work shirt and blue jeans flew by and bounced around the shop like a pinball. On the next bounce Andy caught him, also by the scruff of the neck, and spun him around to face me. "This heah my otha boy, boss, Randy. They twins but ain't 'zactly the same, as you kin see. Randy, say hey to the boss heah." In a voice similar to the one I had just heard in the previous introduction Randy also squeaked out, "Hey, boss." He was built like his brother, but he had a darker complexion and jet-black hair. They must have chosen the same hairstylist as Randy had the same unkempt bushy hairdo as his brother.

Andy dropped the boy and half whispered to me, "Thet one, he got lotsa energy. We thank may be somethin' wrong with him so we make him kinda ass-is-tant to ever'body. Someone needs somethin', he gets it fo' 'em. He a good worker, he just cain't pay 'tenshun fo' too long."

We moved on to a bright red 1962 Volkswagen Karmann Ghia convertible whose trunk lid was partially open. The trunk on the Volkswagen was located in the front of the car as the engine was behind the passenger compartment. As we rounded the front of the little sports car we spotted two legs sticking out of the opening with the lid closed down on them. Andy looked at the motionless legs and lifted the trunk lid up all the way. Lying facedown, in a fully prone position, was a man who looked to be in his early twenties. He had short blond hair and a medium yet sturdy build, and appeared, although I could see only half of his face, to be a rather good-looking young man. He was fast asleep.

"This here's Cousin Jamey, boss. He got a dis-order a some kind. You be talkin' ta him an if ya don't watch it; he'll sure fall asleep on ya. He's a good worker, don' worry, he'll mostly wake on up in a minute an' get back ta work. Neva 'members a thang when he wakes up, neva knowed he was out. Doc says not fer us ta wake him, so's best jes to leave him be."

"You mean we just leave him there, fast asleep?" I asked. "He gets paid to sleep in the trunk of a car?"

"Piecework, boss, piecework. He git paid wot he does, jes like us all. Look, boss, he comin' 'roun'."

The man didn't move, but his eyes opened wide and he looked startled. He turned his head, looked down, and started cleaning with the rag that had never left his hand.

"See," Andy said, "never knew what happened."

Andy used his scruff of the neck grab and pulled him straight up out of the trunk. I was amazed at the man's strength.

"Jamey, this is the boss, say hey to him."

"Hey, boss," he said as ordered. Except for Andy, the Calhoun's appeared to be men of few words. Andy proceeded to then carefully grab him by the belt loop and collar and lift him back into the trunk carefully placing him in the same position he had previously occupied.

Andy motioned me next to a 1964 four-door Ford Falcon, white, with a powder-blue interior. The rear seat had been removed and sat next to the car while a vacuum cleaner hummed close by. Two more legs protruded from the right rear door giving proof that someone was cleaning the interior. I prepared this time for Andy to grab the man again by the scruff of the neck and introduce me to him, but instead Andy flipped off the vacuum cleaner with a deft move and, to my surprise, called gently into the passenger compartment of the smallish Ford. "Elle, Bugbear, come on up outta theah. I wont ya ta meet somebody."

The person inside backed out of the car and turned toward us.

"Boss," Andy said, "this heah's ma wafe, Elle, she a in-tear-eor spesh-ill-ist. Woman can do six in-tear-eors a day by her own self, she can. Elle, this here's the boss."

"How do you do, ma'am?" I said. "It looks like you're doing a good job there."

Andy's wife was a huge contrast to him. She would only come up to Andy's armpits if she could stand up straight, and her frame was thin and wiry. Her hands were full of sponge and soap and she had worked up a good sweat, some of it dripping on my shoes as we spoke. Her stringy hair was all tied up into a mop on top of her head by a red kerchief. She wore, of course, a blue work shirt and dark blue jeans two sizes too big for her skinny little legs. I knew right away, this was no woman to toy with.

"Ah'm doin' these here in-ter-iors all my lafe," she said. "Ah'm fas', an Ah'm good. You don't neva need ta look ova ma work. It's jes raght, alla the tame. Got it?" She said all this in a manner that no one would want to argue with, certainly not me. She then turned to Andy with an angry look on her face.

"Andrew," she chastised him, "we almost done here, you got anuther car to do or ain't we? Ah's sittin' on my rear end waiting around for you ta finish that po-lish" ---- yes, like the country— "job, now git to it, or Ah'm goin' home."

Andy's smile turned serious.

"Yas, deah," he replied, "you raght, Ah'm getting' raght back on thet polish job. Ye can hev it lickity-split, suga'."

Elle, I could tell, was suspicious of me.

"Nace to meet ya, *boss*," she said. She then dove into the rear seat of the car and went back to work. Andy whispered in my ear, "She's a fane woman she is, jes don' eva git on her bad sade. She got her own opinions, thet for sure, but she a fane woman and a fane worker."

Andy did as he was told and went back to work on his polish job. As I walked back to the office I noticed the trunk lid on the Pontiac he was working on moving up and down so I looked to see what the problem was. I pulled the lid open only to find another stranger, a woman I thought, in the trunk. She had a bottle of all-purpose cleaner in one hand, and a rag in the other. She had short gray hair and was a smaller and much older version of Elle. She was toothless and wore small oval eyeglasses that had a homemade cord attached to prevent them from falling off. A faded gingham dress was barely showing underneath one of Andy's work shirts that reached all the way down to her button-top shoes.

"Who the hell'er you!" she yelled at my face. "Yer scared the livin' shit outta me, boy!"

She extracted herself from the trunk and gathered herself up in front of me. She was even smaller than Elle, an elf of an old woman.

"So sorry, ma'am, I didn't know you were in there."

"You little shit, where else would I be? Makin' hotcakes? Who the hell are you anaway, shithead?"

"I'm Steven," I said. "Who are you?"

"Wail Ah'm Granny, shithead," she bellowed. "What the hell you want?"

"I-I-I'm trying to meet everyone, I'm the owner here, Steven Reilly."

"Ah don' give a bird shit who owns what aroun' here, sonny. Ah works for ma young'un Elle, thet's all I knows, now git yo' skinny shit self outta heah and let me be doing ma work."

With that she waved me off, and I quickly learned to give Granny a wide berth.

I walked over to Andy, who was standing on a stool polishing the roof of the car he was working on. He flipped the buffer off and looked down at me.

"I see ya done met Granny," he said.

"Yeah, she sure says *shit* a lot."

"Oh, don' you worry none 'bout Granny, she's harmless. She gots a bark, but she ain't got no teeth to bite with no more."

"Andy, these people are never going to listen to what Herb or I say. How are we going to control the work?"

"Now looky here, you the boss, but ma family does what Ah tells 'em. You an Herb tell me, an' I tell them what ta do. The work gits done an ever'one is happy. Don't worry, boss, ever'thang is gonna be jes fane."

Andy stepped off the stool, looked around, and then moved closer to my face.

"Say, boss," he whispered, "does the Roach come 'round heah? Ah heared Herb is a fren a his. Ah gots somethin' fer him if'n you see him."

"Sure thing, Andy," I replied, pretending to know what he was talking about.

Who was this phantom "Roach" everyone knew about except me?

Was he important? I wasn't going to let it worry me, but he was always in the back of my mind.

I sat in my office and looked around my little kingdom. Work *was* getting done, and we *would* clean twice as many cars as we did before Andy and his family arrived. My greed kicked in and I lost my misgivings; the Calhoun's were here to stay.

Chapter Eleven

BRAWLIN'

I had created a new business model. The Calhoun clan served as a subcontracting company to Reilly Detail, with Andy and Elle behind the scenes directing all work performed by the family. Every morning Andy's old 1956 Chevy panel van pulled up and the entire family exploded out of the big double doors to pounce on any work left over from the day before.

As promised, I paid them only for the jobs that were completed. Andy shuttled Granny and Elle home in the afternoon when they were no longer needed. I didn't care about their peculiarities or hours worked as I was paying everyone on commission. It no longer bothered me to walk by Jamey fast asleep in the trunk or in the back seat of a car. No one seemed to notice, and everyone was careful not to wake him up.

Sandy and Randy, however, developed a disturbing pattern: they seemed to enjoy a good fight. About once a day, on average—it wasn't uncommon for two or three to break out in a day—one of them would cross the other, and sure enough, a fight would ensue. Neither a verbal sparring match, nor even a good shoving match; these were all-out brawls.

At break time, as we sat around drinking our coffee or making fun of Hector the lunch truck guy, the two boys would joke with us, laugh, and join in on the camaraderie. At any moment, however, a wrong word could be spoken, a shove given, and all hell would break loose. The first time it happened I was shocked by the display, but by the third or fourth time I just watched it with the same curiosity as on Friday nights when Dick Lane called a wrestling match between Gorgeous George and the Destroyer.

Fists flew; there was kicking, gouging, ripping of clothes, and a fair amount of cursing. Nothing was illegal, and there was no referee. The matches ended quickly, rounds lasting about one and a half minutes. This was around the time it took Andy to figure out there was a fight occurring, turn his polisher off, and then arrive at the scene of the fisticuffs. Andy would pick up one teenager, then the other, by the scruff of the neck and command them in exactly the same voice every time.

"Stop faghtin'! This is *work*; this ain't play. Ah'm gonna whack you both good you don't get back ta work."

Often the boys continued flailing as he held them up in the air, and I found this part of the fight as interesting as the fight itself. The combatants now had a choice: cease hostilities, or be taken by the shirt collar to the back of the shop where Andy pinned them against the concrete wall until they calmed down. I was amazed that when the flailing and cursing stopped, everyone went back to work as if nothing had happened, and at the next break both boys were best friends again. Other than a few bruises, a bloody nose, or a ripped shirt, it was as if the fight never took place. Through every pugilistic episode Granny and Elle never looked up from their work. They acted as if this was normal behavior, which in West Virginia, it might have been. Jamey slept right through it.

The afternoon after the first big fight, Herb, Andy, Jack, and I were delivering a light blue four-cylinder 1964 Chevy Nova two-door sedan back to Doug Schultz. I was, of course, driving, but today's fight was still on my mind.

"Those kids were fighting for real Andy," I said. "What's that all about? They seem OK with each other most of the time, but they were out for blood today."

"Aw, they's jes kids. Kids lak ta faght. Them kids got their momma's temper, thet for sure. One minute she fane, next she whuppin' my ass.

Don' ya worry, Ah keep them kids in lan. They don' cross Pappy; if'n they do, they got ta ansa ta momma, and thet, boy, ain't no fun."

"Yassuh," Herb joined in, "Those boys sho got some fi-ya in the belly, that fo' sho. If someone teach 'em how ta faght proper, they hoit theysel's fo' sho."

"Oh, they faghts West 'Ginny style all right," Andy replied. "Anathang goes, but careful of the privates. Ah seen growed men faght fer hours thet way, best frens maght be. Man's gotta wrestle it out sometame, thet jes the way it is."

"Yas, I suppose you right," Herb said. "Man, he sometame got to de-fend hisself. I don' much lak it ma-self, Ah'm a lova, not a faghta. Got ma-self in a couple a scrapples back in Chee-ca-go. Man got to learn to de-fend hisself. You ever been in a scrapple, boy?"

"Naw, not really," I replied. "A few kid fights, but that's about it. I don't have time to get into any fights; wouldn't know what to do if I did."

"Look, boss," Andy said, "you just got to larn one thang 'bout faghtin'; you got to get mad, real mad. A crazy-mad man will beat anotha man ever' tame. You just got ta get mad an' start swinging, kickin', an bitin'."

"Naw, tha's ain't winnin' no faght," Herb replied to him. "Tha's redneck cracker brawlin', tha's all it is. Bes' faghts be showt faghts. Man got to be quick; man got to give the fust blow. Betta yet, they's real trouble, you best get you a blade for pro-tec-shun."

"Tha's nigger fighting, tha's all that is," Andy responded. "You all wanna jes cut each otha up tha's fane, but that ain't no fair faght."

I noticed that Herb did not take offense at Andy's remarks; neither did Andy at Herb's. The terms they used shocked me, but then I realized they were not inflicting the slurs on each other, only on the particular method of fighting. The crude talk seemed acceptable to each of them.

I looked in the rearview mirror at Jack. He knew we were talking about fighting, but the subtleties of the conversation escaped him. I felt sorry for him, so I tried to bring him into the discussion.

"You ever get in a fight, Jack?" I asked him.

"Oh yeah," he responded, "a couple times I got hassled, one time at the Clown man."

"What happened?"

Herb and Andy were silent now and paid close attention to his answer, hoping to decipher it without interpretation.

"This big dude," he began, "used to come into the drive-through with his comrades. I think he was a jock dude from Santa Ana Junior College, nasty sorta dude. One time the punk whiffed me by takin' his greasewich prior to coin exchange an' then gave me the ugly stick, middle finger, ya know. Uncool man, it really toasted my rocks man. I was bummed out man. You know, really mad, mad like Festus here said ya gotta be."

Jack called Andy "Festus" sometimes because he talked like the character from the Western TV show *Gunsmoke*, looked a little like him too. Andy didn't seem to mind; he thought Jack was a quart low in the brain department anyway.

"I don't know what happened to me man," he continued, "but this cat really flipped me out."

By the look on the other faces in the car, I figured I better intervene with a comprehensive interpretation.

"A big football player came into Jack's work and didn't pay for his food," I translated. "What did you do then?" I asked Jack.

"Wow man, it was really weird. I spazzed out and Frisbeed him with a fried pie." He said it casually, as if this were an everyday occurrence.

"What!" I replied. "Even *I* don't understand what you're talking about."

"Well man," he explained, "me and Squeaky, you know, the chick I work with sometimes, the one with the big titties, we sometimes play Frisbee with the fried pies."

"What's a Frisbee?" I asked him.

"Oh man, they're so cool. The dude that invented the Hula-Hoop put forth this twitchin' plastic thing that looks like a flyin' saucer except instead of bein' as big as a house it's like the size of four fried Clown pies stuck together."

He looked at Andy sitting next to him in the back seat and mistook the confused look on his face for one of logical questioning.

"A Hula-Hoop is the thing you wear on your ass man," he said to Andy. "You know, you swing it around so's it stays up on your ass. Some reason, it works better on kaak, chicks, you know, probably 'cause they got bigger asses than guys."

Andy's mouth was open as if he was going to say something, but he didn't know where to start and faltered. Jack, thinking Andy understood him, continued: "So Squeaky and I figured out you could toss a fried pie kinda like one of those Frisbees, 'cause they are kinda flat and fried hard on the outside cause you drop 'em in the French fry grease. You sorta flick the little turds with your wrist and they, like, spin man. After closin' sometimes we played this groovy game and spin pies at the plastic clown in the drive-through—see if we could get one in his mouth, you know?"

"Jack," I interrupted, "what has any of this got to do with fighting?"

"Hey man, I was gettin' to that. Well, this big dude that I really was pissed at 'cause he was always throwin' shit at my own self through the window stiffs my dick for the scratch and I flip out like Festus' here kids do sometimes. I snatched up a fried pie and Frisbeed it right out the window and hit the ratfink, smack, right in his jawbone. It was kinda far out; the pie explodes in the dude's face and little bits of pie goo fly all over his car and all over his big dude friends. Well the fat turd has a cow over the whole thing and proceeds to jump outta the car and run for the walk-in door to the Clown. I vocalize in a big way that someone needs to lock the door and, fortunate for the Jack here, Squeaky hears me man. She gets a key in the door just before the dudes hit it full speed. I call the pigs, they show up and catch the guys tryin' to kick in the nose of the plastic clown and bust 'em. Bummer was; I had to clean the plastic clown after they had hocked lugies all over it. It was groady, man."

"*That* was your fight?" I said.

"Yea, *brutal* man, you shoulda seen it, freaked me out." he replied.

I was trying to figure out what to tell Herb and Andy about Jack's story. There wasn't enough time to interpret the whole story, and I wasn't sure I could make sense out of it anyway.

"Jack had a fight with the big guy; the cops came and took the guy and his friends away," was my edited version.

Both Andy and Herb smiled at that, nodding in semi-acknowledgement.

Silence prevailed as we all tried to make our own sense out of Jack's story. A few minutes passed before Herb felt as though he had something important to say.

"Most impo'tant thang you boys need to know 'bout faghts is the rules," he said.

"What rules?" I asked.

"Wail," he began, holding up a finger for each rule.

"*Rule one*: If'n a man got a blade, give him wot he want an' run.

Rule two: If he got a gun, run fasta.

Rule tree: If you got a blade, he got a blade, cuts an' run. You all heard the sayin' 'cuts an' run'? Tha's what it mean.

Rule fo': If a man yo' size got no blade o' gun, hit him ha'd inna stomach 'fo' he has tame to hit you. When he bend ova breaving heavy, walk away.

Rule fave: Man bigga en you, you got no chance, you kick him ha'd as you kin, raght in his man-hoods. *Then* you run."

"Sound lak a lot a runnin' ta me," Andy commented.

"Dese boys, lak me, Andy, they lovas, not faghtas. Wot I tell them keep them safe, tha's all. They not gonna be no Rocky Mar-key-ano, they jes need not ta get theyself all busted up. One mo' thang, you boys, some men, bad men, you don' mess with, nohow, no tame. This kinda man, you jes stay away from."

"Like who you talkin' about, Herb?" I asked. "What kinda man?"

Herb would not answer.

"Lak, the Roach kinda man," Andy declared.

Herb just nodded.

Herb made us repeat the rules back to him. Jack had a hard time with the number of rules, so I condensed them for him.

"Just remember," I told him, "rule *five*: kick 'em in the nuts and run."

Herb made us repeat rule five twice, then added, "You got to kick 'em lak you wont that dick onna *inside* 'stead a ona *outside*, unnerstan'?"

"Yeah," we both said while feeling an uncomfortable twinge deep in our netherlands. "We got it."

Chapter Twelve

THE ROACH

I was inspecting a 1960 Mercury Comet one morning just prior to delivery when I saw a car pull up on the side street behind the shop. It was a striking automobile, a jet-black 1965 Cadillac Coupe de Ville. A glitzy car to begin with, this one had big fat whitewall tires that complemented the bright chrome wire wheel hubcaps. It was spotless, so clean I could see the mint green leaves on the maple tree across the street mirrored in the Caddy's recently polished rooftop. A necklace with what looked like a silver dollar and two white felt dice attached to it hung from the rearview mirror.

A man emerged from the car, a large man. After scanning the lot, he walked straight toward me. Suddenly, the shop went silent, the traffic stopped, and the birds quit chirping as his foot crossed the curb. I was curious at first, then fearful, as he came face-to-face with me.

Not waiting for me to speak, he questioned me with a deep, somber voice: "Wheah is 'Erb?" was all he said.

The sunlight reflected off his silver belt buckle and caught me in the eye; I blinked as I tried to get a good look at him.

"Inside," I replied.

"Get him, tell him Eddie Roché is here."

He looked right through me; I was invisible to him.

I found Herb under the hood of a 1958 Ford pickup truck.

"Herb," I told him, "there's a *man* out here wants to see you."

Herb looked nonplussed.

"He said his name is Eddie."

Herb quickly came to attention, stood up straight, and tried to clean himself up with a shop rag as best he could.

He walked out to meet the visitor, with me close behind. Herb forced a smile as he approached the man and stuck out his half-clean hand.

"Hi, Eddie," he greeted him.

The stranger shook his hand, but his expression never changed. I was to find out his expression *never* changed. "'Erbert, how *is* you?" he replied.

"Fane, jes fane," Herb said. "Ever'thang gooood, we doin' fane."

I was standing directly behind Herb and just to his side like an attachment. I had to find out who this guy was. Herb's elbow hit my chest on the downswing from his handshake and he could no longer ignore me.

"Oh, this here's the chief, man what owns the shop, Mista Steven. Steven, this here is Eddie Ro-shay. Eddie here is a biz-ness potna. He a succ-ses-ful biz-ness-man an' a good fren."

Eddie had his hands in his pockets as he rolled a toothpick around his perfect pearly-white dentures. I was either too unimportant, or too young, for him to shake hands with.

"We got some biz-ness to care about, boy," Herb said to me, "Ah'll be back in a while."

With that Herb got into Eddie's Cadillac and they took off.

I walked back with none of my questions answered and slightly annoyed at the way I had been treated by them both. Speed was sitting in the office by himself, blowing into a big white coffee cup adorned by bright red English script down the side indicating the giftor of said cup. "LANCE-A-LOT" it read. Often midmorning he would take the remainder of his sugar-slurried coffee and pour it from the cardboard Winkel's cup into this, his favorite ceramic mug. He would then heat it up on the engine manifold of a client's car. This was his break.

I walked into the office, closed the door, turned a chair around backwards, sat, and faced Speed. He looked up at me; he knew he was cornered. Speed was always uncomfortable in one-on-one meetings with the door closed; he had learned the hard way that they often turned out badly.

"Who was that guy, Dave?" I asked him.

"Daid not see him, Mista Steven, what he look lak?"

"He was a big man, well-dressed. He had a black linen shirt with a white ascot around his neck. His hair was black; slicked back. He had on alligator shoes and his belt buckle almost blinded me."

"Waal, ain't you Perr-y fu-ckin' Mason, Mista Steven. Does all you white boys notice ever'thang 'bout otha men?"

"I was *curious*, that's all. We don't get too many well-dressed men driving Cadillacs in here looking for Herb."

"Was he kinda scowly? Daid he hev a slicky-lookin' moos-tache?"

"Yeah, he did. Who is the guy Dave?"

"Waal, es none yo' biz-ness what man 'Erbert meet with, an you don' need be askin' questions. I tell you here only 'cause you got ta watch out for this man. He is the Roach, Eddie the Roach."

"What's he got to do with Herb?" I asked him.

"Wail now, ag'in," he continued, "is none yo' biz-ness, but you best know that man be daaaangerous. You know, 'Erbert, he plays the ponies, es his weak-a-ness. 'Erbert a good man, but all men got a weak-a-ness. The ponies es 'Erbert's. Some men take to drink, some to poosy, some even beats the wife; 'Erbert a good man, don' do none a that, but he *do* lak the ponies. That Roach; he es a *boogie*. You know what that is, Mista Steven?"

"Yeah, I think so, he takes bets. From the looks of him, he's pretty good at it."

"Thas raght. He take bets, sometames big ol' bets. You bet with the Roach you betta has the cash ta back it up. 'Erbert thinks he knows them ponies so's he bets 'em, sometame he win, sometame he lose. When he win, he think he going to win all the tame. Not true, Mista Steven, gamblin' jes make the boogie money, never makes no one else money. You see the car he drivin', Mista Steven?"

"Yeah, it was a good-lookin' Cadillac."

"I give the last two teef in my mouf fo' that car. You see, Mista Steven, I don' wanna get no money by nobody's mis-er-ee. Tha's why they calls him the Roach: he feed off other people's mis-er-ee. Lakwise, you cain't kill a roach. Ah heard many men have tried ta kill this one, none was able. Ah wont you ta stay away from that man. You don' let 'Erbert know we talked 'bout him neither. 'Erbert goes his own way, got his own prade, ain't for us to nose around en his biz-ness."

"OK, Dave, I get it. I just worry about him. What if he gets in trouble? He doesn't need to hang around men like that."

"You too young to worry so much, Mista Steven. 'Erbert, he takes care of hisself. Speed here watch out for 'Erbert, always do."

The black Cadillac pulled up and we watched Herb get out. I stood up and put my hand on the doorknob to leave but then turned back and looked at Speed.

"Dave," I asked him, "what are *your* weaknesses?"

He looked up, then down at his open palms. The whites of his eyes had turned a dirty yellow over the years. I knew those eyes and the dark lines on his face held many deep secrets. He heaved a great sigh of resignation.

"When Ah's a young man, Ah tasted 'em *all*, son. Cain't say Ah was a good man, nor even no honest man like 'Erbert. But thas a looong tame ago. Now ma weakness be watching too much a telebision ever' naght. White men doing crazy thangs on thet telebision, but thet's all Ah got now, an all Ah wont. Age catch up to ol' Speed. Young men lak youse, it's yo' tame. Be you careful watchya do with that tame, it be gone soon. Don' wanna wind up like ol' Speed, some worn out ol' man. Keeps yo' weakness unna control boy, and you be a happy man."

"You're a good man, Dave," I told him. "Herb's lucky to have you for a friend."

Speed looked up, sweetly, into my face.

"You ma fren too, Mista Steven. We gonna make a good man outta you yet."

I smiled at him, a real smile, a genuine smile. Deep down I felt a true affection for the man. He was a leathery old storybook of life experiences that I had just begun to open up.

"Get back to work, Speed," I told him. "Your breaks are gettin' too long."

"Sheeeeeeeeeeeeeeeiiit," he growled at me.

Chapter Thirteen

LEAN INTO IT

As much as I disliked cleaning interiors, I detested polishing a car. It was difficult, messy work. The machine was heavy and cumbersome. If you pushed on it too hard, it could take the paint off the car and if your pressure was too light, your work was wasted and had to be repeated all over again.

I was stuck one morning polishing an old yellow 1957 Chrysler 300, a behemoth of an automobile that looked as if it had never seen the inside of a garage in its entire life. It had faded to a dingy brownish orange, about the same color as Andy's teeth. I was struggling with the buffer, trying to polish out the many years of neglect, when Herb walked by and studied my work.

"Looks like a zebra, boy," he said. "Ah don' thank yo' daddy wont a striped car."

I stood back and looked at the side of the old Chrysler: it was unevenly polished where I had misapplied the pressure. On a newer car you could get away with bad technique, but on an old oxidized car like this, it looked like bad wall art.

"Man, this is a tough one, Herb," I said. "I hate polishing these old pieces of shit."

"What is yo' thang, boy?" he replied. "You come in here sometame an' got the wors' face on you, lak you hate woiking. Ever'thang a big pro'lem with you. You ought be happy jes ta be alive, boy. Woik is *good* if you lak it; if you don', then best you do somethin' else."

"You tellin' me you enjoy polishing cars?"

"Yassah, Ah do. Ah don' look at it lak po-lishin' no car, boy. Ah look at it lak Ah'm gettin' me some poosy. This heah ca', Ah got to win 'er ova, jes lak a good-lookin' woman. You got to make love to her, slow dance with her, ca-*ress* her. No one got no women, an' they ain't gonna po-lish no car proper, by pushin' an shovin' like you. Watch the 'Erb now, son."

He picked up the buffer and turned it on in one motion. Gently, he glided the machine across the sprawling trunk lid. He moved it deftly back and forth while the subtle movements of his body allowed him to put just the right amount of pressure to the spot he was working on. I stood back and took in the dance of man and car. He sang a soft, high-pitched tune that accompanied the dance, a blues song I could not identify.

He turned the buffer off, and then handed it to me. "Now you try it, boy."

I grabbed the machine, turned it on, and attacked the car. I was clumsy, and my body wouldn't respond to the instructions my mind was giving it. Frustrated, I was ready to give up.

"Boy," Herb said, "don' you care 'bout doin' nothin' raght?"

"What do you mean?" I asked him.

"You neva gonna do anathang raght if'n you don' lak doin' it. Did you neva lak somethin' a lot? Somethin' makes yo' happy insade? Somethin' that yo' extree good at? Mus' be *somethin'*?"

He looked into my eyes and waited for an answer. I was at a loss. He made me think about, and search for, feelings I could never admit to. There was only one thing that came to mind.

"Baseball," I replied. "That's all I've ever been good at: baseball."

"Ah dadn't know you a ball playa, boy. Was you good?"

"Yeah, I was good, I was *real* good; always one of the best on my team. Little league, grammar school, I loved baseball."

"Why you quit playin'? You good at somethin' you need to keep at it."

"I had to go to work. My dad told me I was on my own, moneywise. I couldn't play and work, that's just the way it was."

"Well you gots ta fan somethin' else to love, boy. Lafe will give ya mo' chances. Now pick up that buffa an po-lish that car like you making love to a woman!"

I picked up the buffer again and began to polish. I felt lighter on my feet this time, unburdened a little bit by having vocalized to Herb what was a simple truth: I had given up the one thing I loved in life to work in a shitty detail shop.

"*Lean* into it, boy," he yelled over the whine of the machine. "Anathang you wanna be good at, you got to *lean* into it, give it ever'thang you got."

I started to sing, like Herb would. The first thing that came to my mind as I worked the buffer was the Chuck Berry song, Johnny B Goode.

I had heard the song so many times on Speed's radio the lyrics had become embedded in my brain. Without even a thought, I spit all the words out using the loud hum of the buffer as my background music.

"Go, I yelled out, "Go Johnny Go!"

"Now youse got it, boy," Herb yelled from behind me, "sing to that woman, make that wo-man scream fo' mo'."

Speed, who was working on a car next to me, dropped his buffer and walked in front of the car I was working on so I could see him. He crouched as low as his old body would allow him and snapped his fingers.

The Calhoun's were all looking at us now, Herb and Speed were both snapping their fingers as we all sang the chorus,

> *Go, go, go, go Johnny go*
> *Go, ----- Johnny B. Goode*

Herb smiled and left me to finish my job and sing my song.

I never looked at work the same way after that, then again, I never looked at *anything* the same way after that.

As I moved effortlessly to the front fender, my buffer felt lighter than ever and it fairly glided over the faded yellow paint. The chrome side molding that protected the fender along that side of the car was loose, however, at the very tip. I didn't see it in time and the buffer pad slid underneath the molding, ripping it off of the fender. There was a stab of pain as the sharp rear edge of the molding flew up and hit me in the face. I dropped the buffer and fell backward on the concrete floor.

Speed saw what had happened out of the corner of his eye and ran over to help. He turned off the gyrating buffer now on the floor and grabbed me by the shoulders. Lifting me up to a standing position he held my chin and lifted my face.

"*Shhhheeeeeeeiiit,*" was his astute observation.

My vision blurred as Herb came running over to check on me.

"*Sheeeeeeiit,*" Herb reiterated, as he looked at my mangled face. "Speed, quick, get us some clean rags." I looked down, blood was pouring from my face and onto the floor of the garage.

Herb took the rags from Speed and applied them to my face. He had me lie on the floor of the office while he tried to stop the bleeding.

"How bad is it?" I asked.

"You bleedin' pretty good," Herb replied. "Ah cain't tell how bad yo' eye is cause they's too much blood. You hurtin', boy?"

"It's startin' to throb. I can't see out of that eye at all. What happened?"

"Po-lish man's wust night-mare, boy. Loose chrome pop up an' bitcha inna face. Weren't so bad 'cept hit you inna eye. I got ta take ya to the hos-pital, boy, keep this rag on yo' face."

I looked up with my one good eye: the Calhoun's were all standing around me with sickly looks on their faces. Andy was missing, and I found out why as he pulled up his old van to the office door. The Calhoun boys put me into the back seat and Herb jumped in while Andy drove us to the hospital.

*****

"We need a release to work on this boy," the nurse shouted out as she swept into the room. "He is *not* eighteen; he needs a *parent* to sign a release."

She was a stout woman with a plump face and short dirty-blond hair crowned by a pure white nurse's hat that had little wings on the top. She reminded me of Sister Josephine, the principal who took no shit back in grammar school. I was lying in a bed somewhere in the bowels of the emergency ward at Fullerton Memorial Hospital. Andy was on one side of the bed and Herb on the other. Someone had given me a large pad and an ice pack to hold over my eye, which had since stopped bleeding. The nurse looked wickedly at Herb and then at Andy.

Staring at Andy, she accosted him with a single gnarly finger: "You his father?"

Andy froze; the woman terrified him. Herb nodded his head up and down toward Andy with a silent message to say yes to her.

"Ah, Ah, Ah ain't sure, ma'am," he choked out.

"Not sure," she shrieked, "how are you not sure?"

Herb shook his head in disgust at Andy and looked down, head in hand.

"Waal, I gotta lotto kids, ma'am," Andy told her, "an' this one's got blood all o'er his face. Kin Ah thank about it fer a minute 'r two?"

She looked back at Herb, having decided he was the one in charge. "I will need identification! I doubt *that* man is the father, and *you*, sir, are certainly not! We will not work on this boy until we get a parental release signed."

I was half-conscious, high on the morphine shot they had given me, and saw only comedy in the situation.

I turned my good eye to Herb and reached out to him with my left arm. "Daddy, Daddy, is that you, Daddy? I'm in pain, Daddy. I can't see; where's Momma, Daddy?"

The nurse did not care for my performance. Her hope of throwing us out into the street was nearing fruition and she would not be deterred. "Doesn't look like we have a responsible party anywhere in this room, does it? We may have to send you boys home."

Herb's temper had a slow fuse on it. You didn't, however, want to be around when it ran its course, as the nurse was about to find out.

"Lady," he called out as he stood up to address her, "the boy woiks fo' me. Ah is his *boss*. *Ah* is re-sponsible fo' the boy when he at woik. *Ah* sign the form, *Ah* is re-sponsible, unnerstan'? Now, youse get you ugly ass a doctor in here raght now, a good un, else me an' ma *dumb-ass* pa'tner heah goin' to tear this place apa't."

Her expression changed, and her voice dropped about ten octaves. "Well," she replied, "that's all I was asking for, you don't need to get snippety. Sign here, please."

He did so with a masterful stroke and she left the room.

"Did you try to call my parents?" I asked Herb.

"Ah try to call 'em. Yo' momma don' pick up an' Ah lef a message fo' yo' daddy."

Around ten minutes later the doctor came in and examined my injuries.

"You cut yourself up pretty good, young man," he told me. "I am going to put a few stitches on your face and that should heal up fine. I am, however, worried about the eye. You need to see a specialist. I don't know if you have done permanent damage to it. Only time will tell."

"Is that expensive?" I asked him.

"What difference does that make, son?" he replied. "It's your *eye*." He looked at Herb. "You make sure he sees a specialist. You understand?"

"Yassuh," was all he said.

Herb approached my bed as the nurse bandaged my eye.

"Yo' daddy called back. He say fo' me to take you home, he busy at woik. You gonna be OK, that eye heal up fo' you, you see."

The look on his face said that might not be true.

"Thanks, Herb. My fault, I should have seen that loose chrome."

"Aw, you got all woiked up singing that song. 'Johnny B. Goode' ain't be so "good" fo' ya afta all."

That night I couldn't sleep. I took three aspirin and washed them down with one of my dad's Olympia beers I had stolen out of the refrigerator. I was lying in bed when I heard the door to my room open; it was Pop.

"Son, you all right?" he asked as he sat alongside me on the bed.

"Yeah, I'm OK," I replied.

"Sorry I couldn't get there today, I was busy."

His breath was hot and boozy.

"That's all right, sir, Herb took me in. We watch out for each other at the shop."

"He told me about your eye, Son. Look, we'll get you a specialist, don't worry about the money, I have insurance at work now."

"That's good, thank you, sir."

I knew there was, down deep, a caring father in his soul somewhere. He would at times like this try to express his feelings for me; it just never came out right.

"Look, Son, life is tough. You got to be even tougher or it will take you down. I know I'm not around like a lot of fathers are, but that's gonna toughen you up, already has. You've learned to take care of yourself, that's more than any of the other kids your age can say. It's a valuable lesson."

"Sir, why don't you like Herb?" I asked him.

"I like Herb," he answered. "Why do you say that?"

"You talk down to him, that's why. He's a good man; he doesn't deserve it. Is it because he's black?"

His droopy eyes opened wide with anger.

"Don't be ridiculous," he called out. "I served with a lot of good black men in the war; heroes, some of them. Don't ever accuse me of prejudice: understand? I just don't think you know what kind of men you are working with over there at that shop. They work hand to mouth, travel from job to job. They live in a different world than you do. You need to be careful and watch your step or they'll take advantage of you and you'll never see them again. White, black, it doesn't make any difference, they're low class, out for themselves. You need to watch your back every minute, Son."

"Herb is a good man," I maintained. "So are Andy and Speed. I'm lucky to have them. A man doesn't need to wear an expensive suit to be a *good* man. I'm beginning to think it's the other way around."

He took offense at the remark, as he should have. He got up from the bed, turned around, and said curtly, "Good night, Son."

I watched him leave. His suit and tie were loose and wrinkled. I looked at the clock: it was two in the morning.

I was cold, physically and spiritually. My eye was throbbing and my dad had left me with an empty feeling. I wondered if becoming a man was worth all the pain it took to get there. A hazy, teenage confusion clogged my mind; life used to be so easy when I was a kid. I fell asleep and tried, very hard, to dream; a comforting dream, a dream of happier times, innocent times.

Chapter Fourteen

GRANDPA REILLY'S

It was a warm summer day back in 1961. My bare feet were on fire from the sizzling concrete but I dared not wear down the metal cleats on my shoes while walking home on the hard sidewalk. My uniform that I loved so much was a size too big for me and I looked lost in it but my uncle said it would have to last me one more year until I grew into it. I had been playing organized baseball ever since I was six years old when my sports-loving uncle Dan enrolled me in a pee-wee league down at the town park. Every summer I reveled in the thrill of playing baseball, real baseball, on a real team, with a real uniform.

They only gave you a T-shirt back then, and I yearned for the day I would turn eleven years old, because at that age I could play in the big leagues: Little League baseball. Little League was a big step up for a young man. The field was grass instead of dirt, and there were organized practices. They had grandstands for the parents to cheer from, concession stands to get a hot dog from after the game, and, best of all; you got a genuine uniform.

Uncle Dan escorted me to our local J. C. Penney store for the first fitting of a real uniform. I'll never forget the feeling I had when I cinched up those white cotton pants with that bright red felt belt.

"You're gonna need some metal cleats," he told me. And off to the sporting goods store we went.

"What position are you going to play, boy?" the young sporting goods salesman with the red bow tie asked me.

"Catcher," I quickly replied.

"You're gonna need a cup, then," he informed me.

"My coach makes us drink a lot of water, mister," I told him. "Says we'll get the cramps otherwise. We got a fountain, though, I don't need a cup."

The salesman looked to Dan for help.

"No," my uncle said, "for protection, Stevie. You got to wear a cup over your groin," he told me as he pointed down at my prepubescent manhood. "Here," he said, grabbing one off the shelf. "Try one on."

It was big enough to cover Sonny Liston's groin, but I did as I was told and slipped it on over my jeans. Uncle Dan gave it a good rap with his knuckles.

"See, Stevie, ain't nothin' gonna get through there. The boys are now protected."

He faced me to a mirror on the wall: the cup looked like a petrified gas mask extending from my navel to about mid-thigh. Thinking Yogi Berra must have had one this big; I could only thank the salesman for his sage advice. Regrettably, as I walked around trying to get used to the giant scrotal protectorate Mrs. Donahue who worked at the nearby Rexall drug store walked by and about fainted when her eight-year-old daughter pointed at my crotch and yelled, "What's that, Mommy?"

So there I was, walking home from a Little League game with my shoes tied together while hanging over my shoulder, my cup resting in my army surplus backpack, as it wouldn't fit in my pocket, and my twenty-eight-inch Louisville Slugger bat in my hand.

I wasn't whistling "Take Me Out to the Ball Game," but I was a pretty happy kid. I was eleven years old, we'd won our game, and I was on the way to Grandpa and Grandma's house.

My house was only five blocks from Town Park and the baseball fields, allowing me to walk or ride my bike there every day during the summer. Halfway home was Grandpa and Grandma Reilly's home, a must-stop for me, and a delightful respite from my own dysfunctional household.

As I approached the old house, I spotted Grandpa up on a ladder painting the white trim over the front door. The house was a craftsman, built just past the turn of the century. My grandparents had raised six boys in the three-bedroom, two-bath house, and thirty-five years later the happy couple was still there. My grandfather was retired; he'd left the navy after twenty years and then tried his hand at the car business, turning a very successful dealership over to my father, who lost it with a series of fatal mistakes.

Most people retire and "downsize" *from* their home. My grandfather retired *to* his. He fancied himself a first-class handyman and a day rarely passed that you wouldn't find him working on that big white house, either painting, cleaning, or repairing something that needed attention. The wonderful thing for me was that Grandpa and Grandma were always home. They were up early every day in order to attend morning mass two blocks away at Saint Catherine's Catholic Church, after which they stopped by the post office and the bank on their way home before settling in to a full of day of work on the venerable old Reilly house.

I climbed up the steps to the massive front porch that welcomed everyone into Reilly-land. There was a rocking chair perched on either side of the hand-hewn mahogany front door, in the middle of which was a tiny leaded-glass window that allowed those inside to identify who was coming to call.

My grandfather lifted his paintbrush away from the house and shouted down at me, "Don'tcha walk unner the ladder, Mickey, it's bad luck, ya know!"

I was careful to walk around the ladder but failed to escape the bad luck he was speaking of as a falling ash from the Camel cigarette that was perpetually dangling from his lips hit me square in the face. Henry Reilly then scampered down from his perch on the ladder above the doorway. He was a very spry sixty-six years old. His dark red hair had by now had turned a light gray; it was always short and neat, having been trimmed once a week for the last thirty years by Stan the barber who also cut the hair of every other man in town. Grandpa was short and wiry but he had a commanding presence, clear blue eyes, and a smile that would draw you right in.

"Come on in, Mickey," he called out in his Midwest Irish-American brogue, "I t'ink yer Grandma's got lunch fer us."

Walking through the massive front door, I was instantly transported from 1961 to around 1925. My grandparents weren't big on change, or spending money unnecessarily. Solid, sometimes uncomfortable, wood furniture they had owned since they were married decorated the formal living room. To the left was the dining room where a massive pine table and twelve matching chairs had hosted a great many family gatherings.

A narrow doorway then led us into the farm-style kitchen that had its own smaller dining area, which was where the real action took place. My grandmother Helen was, to say the least, a superb cook. If any activity were perfected by the time spent in pursuit of the art involved, my grandmother would have been one of the true culinary experts of her time. She was *always* in the kitchen fussing over God knows what on her antique white porcelain stove. Apparently the time she put in cooking allowed her the privilege, or perhaps the duty, of forcing her grandchildren to eat far more than the human body was ever designed to consume.

Chicken and dumplings, cookies and cakes, roast beef and potatoes, pies and ice cream; soups and stews, bread, fruit, vegetables, all homemade, and all prepared fresh every day.

When I was in school, I pulled lunch out of a plain brown bag with my name scrawled on it. Every day it was the same: either peanut butter and jelly or bologna on Weber's white bread, and a bag of Laura Scudder potato chips. Today's lunch at Grandma's house was not quite the same:

A sandwich: freshly roasted chicken on homemade sourdough bread right out of the oven, accented by a piquant rosemary-cranberry sauce.

Soup, of course: vegetable barley with fresh vegetables that had been simmering on the stove all morning.

Fruit: applesauce made from apples picked from the one of the many fruit trees behind the old house.

Dessert: strawberry pie made from scratch with the world's sweetest strawberries, grown by the Tanaka family over on the east side of town, and, oh yes, don't forget the homemade vanilla ice cream to go with it.

I had to eat it all, every bit of it. My grandmother was insulted if I refused to eat everything put in front of me and then ask for more. One day the previous summer, I had eaten so much at Grandma's on the way home from a ball game that my scrawny ten-year-old stomach revolted and I spewed my recently eaten lunch all over the lovely eighteenth-century picnic table Grandpa had lovingly restored and brought into the informal dining room that served as the main eating and conversation area of the house.

Grandma explained to my mother that I probably had a little heatstroke from playing ball that day and not to worry about my throwing up. We all knew better: I had, encouraged by my grandmother, eaten myself into a vomitatious frenzy.

I sat at my usual place at the far end of the old picnic table reserved for guests. My uncle Dan, the last child still living at home, sat next to me on my right. Grandpa sat at his usual place at the head of the table, directly across from me. Tradition necessitated that Grandma eat at the small counter separating the kitchen from the dining area. This was not a matter of caste, but of practicality. She could not leave her duties—cooking, serving, clearing and cleaning—long enough to sit at the table with us. This is not to say she failed to engage in conversation, far from it; she spoke well on any subject, and would do so without hesitation.

She was a petite woman, hunched over from her lifetime of cooking and cleaning. Her love for my grandfather was constantly on display, and as he spoke at the head of the table, she touched him tenderly on the shoulder when on a break from her kitchen chores.

Topics were diverse at that old table and my grandparents always encouraged my opinion.

That day, that lunch, that discussion, I remember well. The conversation would come back to me time and again throughout my lifetime.

Chapter Fifteen

VIN

"How was yer game taday, Mickey?" Grandpa quizzed me as he slathered butter on the thick slice of bread that would soon be plunged into his bowl of hot vegetable soup. When I first started playing baseball, my grandfather had renamed me "Mickey" after his favorite player and fellow Irishman, Mickey Mantle. The moniker stuck, and that was my name in his household long after my playing days were over.

"Good, we won!" I mumbled through a mouthful of chicken sandwich.

"Ah, that's great, Mickey, yer uncle here says yer turnin' out ta be a fine ballplayer. I wud like to see you play sometime; maybe after I paint the house me an' yer Grandma can come see ya play."

I knew that would never happen, they were tied to this big old house, cooking, cleaning, painting, and fixing her up. But that was OK, that was who they were, and what they did.

"Who's yer fav'rit player now, Mickey?" he asked me. "I unnerstan' yer a big Dodger fan, like yer uncle here, he lives 'n' breathes by them Dodgers, don'tcha know."

"Good question, Stevie," my uncle added. "Who *is* your favorite player? I know it has to be an LA Dodger, or at least it had *better* be."

I stuck a bite of sandwich in my mouth, affording myself the time to think through my answer. This *was* an important question.

"Johnny Roseboro!" I blurted out.

I looked around the room. My grandmother nodded admiringly; she had no idea how the game of baseball was played, or who played it. She adored me so much I could have said Jack the Ripper and she would have nodded approvingly.

My uncle gave me a quizzical look, wondering, I thought, how I'd come to that conclusion.

My grandfather simply gave me an honest half smile and matter-of-factly called me out. "Roseboro, he's a *nigger*, ain't he, Mickey?"

Reactions:

Uncle Dan: Looks horrified and covers his face with his hands.

Grandma: Rushes out of the kitchen with a large wooden stirring spoon in her hand and *thwack,* raps Grandpa soundly on the top of his head.

"You don't use that word around the boy, Father!" she scolded him with her plainspoken Midwest tone. "Blacks are blacks, or Negroes. We don't use that other word, isn't that right, young man?"

Me: I was taken aback; however, I *had* heard my grandfather use that term before. I knew to him the words *nigger* and *Negro* were interchangeable. Still, every time he said it I felt a twinge deep in my soul. I now sat upon the horns of a dilemma. Should I join forces with my grandmother and reprimand the man I so respected, or should I back up his linguistic bigotry?

I did neither; I took the coward's way out.

"Roseboro is a catcher," I said to them all. "Catcher is the most important position on the field, my coach says. He's the player in charge of the whole game when you're in the field. *I'm* a catcher. I wanna be like Roseboro."

"Oh, I unnerstan', Mickey," Grandpa replied, "youse gonna be a fine catcher. This Roseboro, I'm sure he's a good fellow. There's lotsa niggers playin' ball now. I'm sure some are jus' fine fellas."

Grandma reappeared from the kitchen and, *thwack,* gave him another direct shot to the small hairless spot on the top of his head.

Grandma, my moral compass in life, had taken me aside one night after a family get-together where my grandfather used the *n*-word and explained the generational and cultural gap between my grandfather and me, and what was, and wasn't, acceptable language. The good sisters at St. Patrick's reinforced her concept in no uncertain terms as I had witnessed a severe ruler-on-knuckle beating post-*n*-word by Sister Josephine to a poor young miscreant circa 1960.

The theory back then went this way: use of the *n*-word by people of that generation could be overlooked if they attended Mass every week and they were good people in everyday life. In defense of my grandfather, I never heard him speak badly of a black person, or even African-Americans as a group. He grew up with the *n*-word; it was as common to him as *African-American* is to me now. I think being called a mick, potato eater, and various other Irish insults had inured him to slurs in general.

"Dad, can't you call them Negroes?" my uncle pleaded. "That term is a nasty slur and everyone thinks you're a bigot when you talk like that."

I was familiar with the *n*-word, but not yet the *b*-word.

Grandpa knew well what the *b*-word meant. He tightened his already small mouth and raised his voice.

"Sure now, ya think I don't like 'em cause a what I call 'em? That what ya think, now do ya? Wail now, I tell ya, a nigger saved me life, he did. Was in the Great War, it was; in the Navy it was. Boiler blows a ring valve right into me head while I be shov'lin coal on the *S.S. Kearsage* it did. You two not be here now, I tell ya, not for that big nigger. Carries me out he does, just before the boiler blows. Woulda killed me, it would. Big fella; called him Tree, they did, but never knew his real name. Heard they give him a cook's job. Better that was than stoking the fire on a boiler, but little it was for savin' a man's life. Always wished I could thank him, never did. Not right not to thank a man fer doin' what he did.

No, a nigger saved me life; an I ain't got nothin' against 'em. He was as good a man as there ever was, wasn't easy what he did, but he done the right thing by me."

Thwack! Thwack! Thwack! Went Grandma's spoon.

In spite of Grandpa's story and Grandma's rationale, the term always struck an uneasy chord in me. I was a little on the sensitive side as a child, but that did not explain my deep feelings on the subject. A more suitable explanation could have been my indoctrination on race by my real mentor on the subject, Mr. Vincent Scully.

*****

Vin Scully, as most people know, was the famous longtime radio and TV broadcaster for the Los Angeles Dodgers. Hardly anyone, including those who don't give a damn about baseball, is ignorant of who he is, or what he does for a living. Before there was a Dodger Stadium, before the team ever moved to Los Angeles, kids my age had their ears glued to the family radio listening to the heroic exploits of their favorite Brooklyn Dodgers players as told in fact and fable by the melodious voice of Vin Scully.

I can't remember the number of hours I spent in my youth listening to every nugget of information and descriptive tales of failure or success spun by that man. I learned, through him, the batting average of every player on the team. I could even recalculate it after every at bat. I could tell you the approximate earned run average of almost every pitcher in the National League. We didn't play the American League teams, so, of course, that was of no importance. I would hang on each poetic word. The commercials seemed interminable: I didn't care about Union Seventy-Six gasoline, or whether we ate Farmer John bacon; give me my Vinnie to comfort and entertain me.

Jackie Robinson was before my time and I can only conjecture, although much has been said, what Vin Scully and his mentor Red Barber's live broadcasts were like during the heyday of integrating Major League Baseball. By the time the Dodgers moved to Los Angeles, however, the league was fully integrated. The African American players had reached, if not superstardom, an elevated status in the world of fandom.

There was no ugly transition for those of my age. We did not experience the hateful bigotry and tribulations of Major League integration. It was just a fact: the LA Dodgers, in my mind, had a star at every position:

> Koufax; a Jew, pitching to:
> Roseboro; the catcher, a black man.
> Gil Hodges; first base, white.
> Charlie Neal; second base, black.
> Junior Gilliam; shortstop, black.
> Daryl Spencer; third base, white.
> The outfield: Wally Moon, white, Willie Davis, black,
> Tommy Davis, black.

Of course many players came and went, too numerous to mention, but the racial makeup always seemed to stay about the same. Walter O'Malley, and Branch Rickey before him, the owners of the team, had helped to usher in a new era in sports. Their credo was: put the best ballplayers on the field regardless of ethnic background.

This was also the way Vin Scully called the game. If you listened to a hundred games a year for five years, and I did, you would never know the color of the players he was talking about. Obviously, I knew the color and nationality of each player as I had every team member's baseball card, each one carefully extracted from a Topps bubble gum wrapper. Better yet, the Dodgers occasionally televised, in full-spectrum black and white, games played in hated San Francisco. Televisions don't lie about skin color.

Listening to Vin on the radio, you would never know the skin color, religious preference, or anything else about the private lives of the players. The only exception to this rule was if it affected the play on the field, such as the time Sandy Koufax refused to pitch on the Jewish holiday of Yom Kippur.

What mattered to Vin was what happened on the field; it was about the game. He would speak glowingly about any player who performed well, but was equally critical of all who did not meet his standards. There were no favorites, and certainly there was never any bias.

The exception to this rule, and I am biased on this myself, was that I think he liked catchers. This may have been his one weakness, but then again, maybe it was because catchers were involved in so many plays he wound up calling their names out more often than the others'. His description of Roseboro batting down a wild pitch or blocking the plate from a runner who was trying to score with his metal spikes up and aimed right at him made me fall in love with both Johnny Roseboro and the position of catcher.

Vin never used the *n*-word, but I also don't remember him using the term *Negro*, or, for that matter, *black, African American, Hispanic, white, blue,* or *brown*. I am sure he must have done so at some point, but if he did, it would have been in the context of, for example, looking back at the Jackie Robinson story.

He was, and is, the best example of color blindness we will ever know. He was a big part of my life growing up. Yes, I had a few good male role models in my childhood, my uncle and my grandfather were examples, but I didn't spend thousands of hours with them as I did with Vin. He taught me how to treat people with respect, knowing the color of a man's skin says nothing about his character, or his potential.

*****

"You should find that man, Grandpa," I said. "Find him and thank him. I'm sure glad he saved your life, I wouldn't like it if you were dead!"

"Ah, Mickey," he sighed, "I tried, but I could not. I think I will thank him in heaven if I make it there, cause fer sure *he* will. No, it will be in heaven, or fer youse ta find his chil'ren and thank 'em fer me."

That was too big a task for me to comprehend. It was not likely I would ever find the children of the man in the story, and I was, after all, only eleven years old. I instead took a huge bite of the strawberry pie and savored this, my brief window of innocence.

Chapter Sixteen

ALIENS

The doctor said I had to stay home for a few days and let my vision clear up before I could go back to work. The only remorse I felt from the forced vacation was that it was still the end of summer and I would miss out on full days at work instead of school. My only companion in the house at the time other than Mom, who was firmly ensconced in her room, was Inga, our Swedish housekeeper.

Grandma Reilly felt badly for my Mom and myself as she knew Pop was rarely home and there was no one to clean the house or cook us meals. She and grandpa decided to pay for Inga to come in and be an acting Mom for the household, and a nursemaid to the real one.

Inga was a mature, matronly, single woman, whom I guessed to be about sixty or so. She had come over from Sweden to visit her family a few years ago and never returned home. Sven, her brother, dropped her off every morning at seven o'clock and then picked her up around seven at night, or whenever she called for him on the telephone.

She was a big, good-natured woman, with a ready smile and a zest for life. Her uniform was an old-fashioned blue print one-piece dress with a white apron snugly tied around it. I always hoped she had several of these identical dresses or that she washed the same one often as I never saw her wear anything else. Her full face was Swedish white and framed with an old-fashioned pageboy hairdo that had turned gray. She was most likely very pretty in her youth, but age had taken its toll.

Inga was my steady date. Every night when I came home from work Inga would pull out two "TV" trays from the dedicated rack in the front hall closet and place them strategically in the living room. The trays were painted tin rectangles just big enough to hold your dinner and a drink. They were supported by skinny round legs that collapsed, thus allowing the trays to fold away for easy storage. The trays became a staple of our household and had replaced our dining room table long ago.

Inga sat in Pop's leather Barc-A-Lounger chair, and I sat on one side of the pink sectional sofa that cornered the far sides of our plain, but comfortable, living room. These choice seats were the two most optimal positions for watching the four hundred pound RCA color television mounted in a walnut cabinet my dad took in trade on a 1958 Edsel back when he was in business.

I liked the westerns; Gunsmoke, Bonanza, and the Rifleman were my favorites, but the networks around that time were canceling them all as the TV executives were looking for a younger audience. I missed them, as it was easy for me to identify with the characters. There were heroes and villains, and you knew exactly who to root for. I was finding out that real life was not as easy to figure out, and the characters in my world were much more complicated than those on TV.

Inga liked the detective shows like Mannix and the FBI, but she especially loved old reruns of Perry Mason. I think she had a thing for Raymond Burr who played the lead role, or then again, maybe she was just enthralled with the TV version of the American justice system.

I was never to find out if Inga was a good cook or not. She had made an incredible discovery one day while shopping down at the Lucky Market just prior to her working for my family: Swanson's TV dinners. A miracle of modern science, they were a blessing for every undomesticated or dysfunctional household in the country. No cooking, no dirty dishes, just heat them up, and your family would enjoy a delicious, if not nutritious, complete meal. My dad gave Inga a couple of twenty dollar bills once a week to go shopping with and Inga would come home with and a loaf of bread, a large jar of "Skippy" peanut butter, a half gallon of milk, a jar of pickled herring, and about thirty of those delicious ready to heat and eat meals.

My favorite was the fried chicken with mashed potatoes; Inga loved the Swiss steak and noodles. While she was busy in the kitchen heating our aluminum foiled dinners in the oven for 30 minutes at 375 degrees, I clicked around the old RCA dial and find our favorite program to watch.

One of my recovery nights, however, was going to be special: we had a guest. As it was now Friday, a fresh episode of the popular new sci-fi program "Star Trek" was on. Jack's parents couldn't afford a color TV and were still content to watch the world go by in black and white, so I had invited him over to our house to watch his favorite program in living color.

Star Trek was not only Jack's favorite program; it was his latest passion. I think he identified with the odd looking characters, and for some reason, he had the notion that the program was based in real science.

Inga waited for Jack to arrive before she prepared our dinner as I told her he would be dining with us.

"Ja-ja mister Jack," she asked him upon his arrival, "you like the chicken or the meat-a-loaf tonight? Stevie like the chicken, he eat most every night."

"Why, I *never* let my meat – loaf, Missus Inga," he replied. "Ha ha ha Stevie, ain't that right man."

"Whatta you want for dinner Jack?" I said dryly.

"I want to eat like Captain Kirk man, I wanna eat meat loaf like no man has dared to eat meat loaf before. I want to venture into outer meat loaf man."

I turned to Inga who had a strange look on her face. She thought Jack came from a country even further away than her own, a place of odd, incomprehensible people.

"Meat loaf for the spaceman Inga," I told her.

Inga put the three dinners in the pre-heated oven and brought out the third TV tray while Jack and I warmed up the television and got ready for the big show.

We had just sat down on the couch together when we heard a soft rap on the front door. Inga, feeling it her duty, ran to the door to see who it was. We saw the door open and there were voices; Inga turned to me.

"Stevie," she called out, "they is a couple men out a here lookin' for yoo, ja, ja, two men, black as night, out here lookin' for ya."

It was Herb and Speedy Dave. When I hurt my eye, I had left my car at the shop as Herb had taken me home that night. Herb and Dave brought the car home after their Friday night domino game.

I opened the door, pushed the rusty screen door out wide, and greeted them. Speed had his captain's hat in his hands and Herb was peeking through the doorway, curious as to what kind of home I lived in. They had cleaned up the best as they could, but they still showed the effects of a hard days work.

"Hi guys," I said, "come on in, Jack's here, we were just going to watch Star Trek on TV."

Dave looked at Herb wanting to know what they should do.

"No, no, no," Herb said, "we should get home, just wonted to git the car to ya."

"No, really," I told him, "come on in."

And with that I grabbed his shoulder and nudged them in. They said nothing as they stood in the front entryway and tried to take in all the sights and sounds of their strange new surroundings. Inga swept up to us and gave them a big Swedish smile.

"This is Inga." I told them, "she helps out around here, you know, with mom and all." - Herb knew of my mother's condition. - "Inga, we have a couple more guests, this is Herb, and this is Dave. The're friends of mine."

"Ja-ja, I am Inga," she began, "you nice lookin' gentlemen, come in please."

She took Dave's hat from him and placed it in the hall closet. Without a thought, she pulled out two more TV trays and set them up in front of the left side of the faded pink sectional across from Jack and I.

"Stoked to see you dudes," Jack called out from behind his TV tray. "Did not know you men was trekkies. Awesome!"

Herb and Dave fumbled with the TV trays while attempting to emulate how Jack and I were seated behind ours. I doubted they had ever seen one of those contraptions before.

"Ja-ja, you gentlemen like a dinner?" Inga asked them.

"Naw, thanks maam," Herb answered for them both. "We done ate a'ready but thank you."

I noticed Dave was smiling at her, wide, with lots of gappy teeth showing. I thought it was somewhat overdone.

"Ja, something ta drink maybe?"

"Yass'm, that would be fane."

Inga left, but returned a few minutes later with the dinners for Jack and me. She carefully placed them on our TV trays with my Mom's quilted hot pads protecting her hands, the foil covering still in place. She then removed the foil on each one revealing a cloud of steam under which lay our sumptuous meals.

"Who won the domino game?" I asked Herb and Dave.

"The Roach," Herb grunted.

"Thas man is the luckiest damn man I eva did know," Dave added. "He mus' cheat, but damn if'n Ah know how."

"He wins 'cause he playin' with oth'a men's money thas why," Herb replied. "Thet chicken-shit domino money don' mean nothing' to him so's he play's loose. Ah'm gonna whup his ass someday, you wait 'n see."

Inga broke up the conversation as she came back from the kitchen with a large oval tin tray on which she had placed refreshments for her new guests. It was our only serving tray and although it had a picture of Santa Claus drinking a Coke on it, no one really cared. She balanced the tray in one hand as she placed the items one at a time with the other on the TV trays in front of Herb and Dave. There was a half glass of Coca-Cola, warm and neat, for each of them alongside a small plate sitting on a happy birthday napkin left over from a party long ago forgotten.

On each plate Inga had placed a single Fig Newton cookie and a half slice of Kraft processed cheese. I assumed that this was the equivalent of a Swedish snack, a biscuit and cheese, American style.

The boys poked a finger at the offering before deciding that it was edible. Dave boldly took a bite of the Fig Newton.

"Mighty tasty Miss Inga," He told her as she was sitting in the Lazy-Boy with her own prepared meal in front of her.

"Thas some jelly in thet biscuit, nace su-prase. Taaaaaasty."

Inga looked at Dave with a slight blush on her face.

"Ja-ja, thank you mister Dave, I didn't make, you know."

"Waal, don' matter to me, fane biscuit maam, thank you. You awful nace to us."

His smile was luminescent, and it lingered on Inga a little too long.

The show was about to begin, and the last commercials were being played, when Jack turned and whispered in my ear: "Man, I think Captain Speed is makin' a play for the Swede."

Jack had by now added "Captain" to Dave's nickname because of the hat he wore. I wondered how many nicknames people could have, and it was getting hard to keep track of them all, but then again, it was completely out of my control.

I poked Jack with my elbow to shut him up. He looked offended but retaliated by reaching into his pocket and pulling out two fake pointy Mr. Spock ears. I didn't think he needed them as his own ears stuck way out from his head, and were quite large to begin with, but it was a tradition of his to mount the fake ears over his own in honor of his favorite character, Mr. Spock.

It was a fine show as Captain Kirk and Spock were battling the evil Klingon's for the ultimate control of outer space.

Herb: "Thas gun don' shoot nothin', how they be killin' each otha?"

Jack: "It's a stun gun dude, it shoots rays man, you can stun or you can kill, pretty bitchin' huh?"

Dave: "Why they killin' those men? Jest 'cause they black n' hairy? Those big men outta be able to beat them skinny whate boys up."

Herb: "Ah sho lakes that fane looking black woman. Ah go to outa space anatame get me some a that.

Jack: "That's Lieutenant Aruhu, I think she and Captain Kirk got a thing going."

Dave: "You cain't get no woman from outa space 'Erbert! Looong way up! Be-side, that whate man look like he gonna get some a that."

Herb: "Had me a woman one tame, she act lak she from outa space. Venus De-long was her name, Venus Fly-trap they call her. Cain't tells you why in mixed comp-ny. Could'a been on television *she* could'a. Naw, that fane TV woman cain't be afta that skinny ass whate man. She need a real man, lake that big black man with the long hair."

Me: "That's a bad guy Herb, he's trying to destroy the universe. And I don't think he's black, he's just an alien."

Herb: "Don' know why they gotta has the black man be bad."

Inga: "Ja-ja, I think so, I am like the black men too, veeery hand-sume."

She looks flirtatiously at Speedy Dave as she says this.

Jack: "Wow, warp speed man, look at that thing go!"

Me: "Warp speed, Jack, you gotta be kidding. There is no such thing, it's just a way to explain how you cross a billion miles in a few days."

Jack: "You don't know nothin' man, all this is real stuff, look it up man. The guy that makes the show is a scientist man, *Rod-Berry*, the guy knows all this shit is for real, he didn't just make it up man."

Jack was convinced this was all real; there was nothing I could do to change his mind. I thought it best to let him live in his fantasy world, it was much more comfortable to him than the real world he lived in.

It was then time for a commercial:

Winston tastes good like a cigarette should.

The commercial made smoking so attractive I thought I could actually smell the smoke blown out of the pretty young ladies mouth on TV. As it turned out, I could; someone *was* smoking. I looked up, towards the kitchen; standing in the entry to the living room was my mother.

She was tall and thin, and she wore a pale blue taffeta bathrobe tied at the waist with a terry cloth belt. Her hair was covered by a white towel pulled around her head like a turban that made me think she had showered. The smoke from the Winston she held between two of the fingers on her right hand swirled in front of her once lovely face. She posed for a moment. It was a rare appearance, and she wanted it to count.

Mom had nothing to do in her room all day long but watch television. I knew this as I was occasionally called in to adjust the big rabbit-ear antennae on the old black-and-white TV set in her bedroom. She watched only soap operas and old movies as far as I could tell. I thought that over the years she had begun to emulate the "B" movie actresses as those were the only women she knew intimately, and they had become her only friends. Hours in front of the black-and-white TV most likely contributed to her seeing herself as living in a "noir" world, somewhat like the one in the old movies she watched over and over.

The gentlemen in the room, Herb and Dave, wanted to stand up in deference to a woman entering the room. The problem with TV trays, however, is that they were not designed for such courtesies and Herb and Dave were trapped. Like the safety arm on a roller coaster that keeps you in the seat, the trays only allowed them to half sit up in a greeting without spilling coke all over Inga's well-scrubbed oak floors. Jack, Inga, and I stared at the TV, trying not to notice she was there.

Gliding across the room towards Herb and Dave, she flicked off her cigarette ash in my now empty dinner tray as she passed by before standing directly in front of them. She posed again, and in her best Marlena Dietrich voice told them who she was:

"*I,* ----- am his *mother.*"

Dave could not speak, but his mouth was wide open. Herb was trying to figure out what to do, but he was not prepared for what was happening.

"Please, ---- ta meet you, --- ma am." He drawled out.

She turned around, as a model on a runway would, and took a few steps before turning again to face the TV. She lowered herself down on the couch between Jack and me; we both had to scoot over to let her in.

I think Jack would have said hello, but he was somewhat afraid of her, as she could be a little surreal when she decided to appear. I was used to it, others, not as much.

Mom then fell silent as she fixated on the television. Occasionally, she blew smoke sideways, at Jack, instead of into the room. Whether his pointy ears had anything to do with how she felt about him I did not know.

"Ah thank we outta go, Speed, it's getting' late." Herb said.

"Yassuh," Dave answered him, "Ah thank you raght 'Erbert, maybe tame ta go."

"No, No," I called out, "you guys stay, the show's not over. The best part's always the ending."

I didn't want them to leave on an awkward note, but there *was* an uneasy silence in the room until I noticed a sound coming from outside the front door. I was glad for the distraction as it caught everyone's attention and changed the mood. It was a key, turning in the lock. The door popped open, it was my father.

Sometimes he would show up when you least expected it. He randomly had a night off and wanted to be home, away from his work, his worries, and his nightclubs. This was one of those nights.

He had a brown trench coat on and a leather briefcase in his hand. It was fairly dark in the room so he did not notice us right away. He put the coat and briefcase in the hall closet, turned around in the entryway, and walked into the room. He took two steps in, stopped, pulled his head back and looked around.

We were all trapped; by our TV trays mostly, but also by the surprise of him walking through the door. Each of us had our own thoughts at the time, and I would not conjecture as to what the others were thinking. I could, however, guess what my father might be thinking.

Starting from his left he would have seen Jack.

What on earth happened to the idiot kid's ears? What is wrong with that kid? Why on earth would a son of mine choose him as a friend and, what the hell is he doing in my house?

There is my wonderful psychotic wife. Who let her out of her room? Why is she out here in her bathrobe and for God's sake what am I supposed to say to her?

There he is, my second son, the one I'm supposed to love like my first, but never have. Why couldn't he be more like my oldest: decisive, smart, knows how the world works just like me? I can't even talk to this one; he lives in his own world.

Herb and Dave? What the hell are they doing here? Did my son invite them, or did they just decide to sponge off of my goodwill and show up uninvited? Old black men are my son's other best friends? How did that happen?

That Swedish hag, sitting in my chair, eating my food? It pains me to even look at her knowing someone else is paying her and I can't do anything about it.

He turned to the glow and studied what was on the screen. He looked at us, then back at the television. Once more he gazed at the television, then looked back at Jack. Jack responded with a forced, goofy smile.

I can only imagine what his thoughts and emotions were back then. Strange aliens from another planet surrounded him, the ones on television, and even stranger, the ones sitting in his living room.

My father grew up in a world without TV trays, without TV dinners, without TV. Knowing my grandparents, he likely sat down to dinner every night at a perfectly set dining room table and after a warm prayer of thanks offered by my grandfather, he would enjoy interesting conversation and a hearty meal cooked by his doting mother. From this all-American cocoon he was sent off to experience the horrors of war and years of bloody combat, depriving him of all the advantages he had grown up with.

When he returned home, his expectations had to be of what he remembered growing up, and what he hoped for in the future. He would be sure of his success, the respect of his peers, money, and a wonderful family to go along with it. He would come home every night in his new car to an adoring wife, his perfect children, and a home cooked meal. They would all sit around the dining room table and listen intently to his tales of heroism in the war and his adventures in taking on the business world. He would see the image of a man sitting in the corner of the room, it was Norman Rockwell, dabbing at his easel as he repainted the faces of one generation to this, the next.

No, that was not the scene that appeared before him. He looked around the living room once again. An idiot, a catatonic wife, a spineless son, two vagrant black men and a foreign hag eating pre-fabricated food on flimsy tin tables while staring at that mindless box of senseless stories and endless ads for crap they would never need.

What happened? Did this happen just yesterday, or was it over the last twenty years? What happened to my life?

He shook his head, side to side, and walked through the room towards the kitchen. I heard the cupboard open and close, I knew which one it was by the sound of it. Ice clinked in a glass and the cupboard opened and closed again. The bedroom door opened, then closed; he was gone.

We all wanted to escape the chill left in the room, so Inga and I said our goodbyes to all of our guests. Dave gave her a sexy wink as he left and she blushed once again, like a little girl. Inga's brother came and picked her up after they had left and I found myself alone with mom. I sat on the couch next to her for a few minutes, but I was tired.

"I'm going to bed Mom, you want me to leave the TV on?" I asked her.

She didn't answer. I thought she wasn't able to verbalize that she really didn't want to go back in her bedroom, with Pop in there, so I just let her be.

I could hear the television from my room; it was on all night.

Chapter Seventeen

SPIN

The warm summer matured into a cool fall and I was back in school for my senior, and final, year at St. James. I was fortunate in that my eye had healed quickly and the specialist said the only residual effect would be cloudiness that shouldn't affect my vision.

Luckily, I had Herb to watch over the shop while I was in school and I could trust him to keep things running smoothly. We made a good team: he worked with the crew cleaning cars all day until I arrived after school, then we would pick up and deliver cars until about seven in the evening.

Occasionally I would experience a rare treat in the form of a particularly interesting car in need of cleaning and ultimate delivery to Doug Schultz Chevrolet. One such car presented itself to me one dreary and rainy morning.

It was a 1965 Pontiac GTO. Light yellow, almost cream colored, with a jet-black vinyl interior. GTO stood for Gran Turismo Obligato, copied from Ferrari's famous GTO racing machines of the early sixties. The age of the muscle car was blooming and General Motors, Ford, and Chrysler were all building powerful engines and stylish cars designed to sell in big numbers to the baby boom generation. These companies were also trying to burnish their images, as they were now competing with the popular British, Italian, and German sports cars that were flooding into the country.

She was a beauty, two years old, but with a fresh detail it looked like a new car. Customized with Keystone magnesium wheels and oversize racing tires, the Pontiac also came with a fake wood steering wheel, bucket seats, and the latest thing in technology, an eight-track stereo tape player with rear speakers. In my teenage car-crazy eyes, it was an absolutely luscious machine. There were, after all, only two things boys of my age *really* cared about: fast cars, and, naturally, the girls you might get by driving them.

The real attraction of the car was on the inside of the engine compartment, not the outside. This baby had a 389-cubic-inch V-8 engine with Tri Power, four-speed transmission, and positraction rear end. In other words, the car hauled ass. The showroom version was so fast, many owners raced them at the drag strip without any modifications whatsoever.

This was a delivery I really looked forward to, a chance to let it all out and see what this incredible machine could do. I would, of course, have passengers: Herb and Andy came along, as we were picking up three more cars on the other side. The only thing that dampened my spirit, and the ground, was a steady Southern California rainfall.

I gathered up my men, Herb in the front seat and Andy in the back as usual. We pulled out of the driveway with just a hint of chirping and the smell of burning rubber coming from those big beautiful racing tires.

"Tha's some powa in this thang, boy, you know how ta handle it?" Herb asked me.

"Are you kidding me?" I replied. "I've driven every car General Motors made in the last two years. SS 396's, Corvettes, Olds 442's, I *am* the closest thing to a professional race driver you'll ever know."

"Ah know *real* race drivers back home," Andy threw in. "Them boys raced on weekends an' run liqa durin' the week. Ain't no one cud touch 'em on er off the track. Them cars was hopped up too, make this here Chevy look like one of them Nazi cars."

"Those are called *Volkswagens*, Andy," I replied, "and this ain't no Chevy, it's a *Pontiac GTO*, and it's a fast, fast car. Let me show you what it can do." And with that I put my foot into the brute and snapped both their heads back enough to get their attention.

"*Sassy* little thang," Herb sang out. "Ah lak the powa, but ah also lak to get home safe, boy."

I backed off the throttle; the car felt pretty skittish on the rainy streets, and it scared me a little.

"Ah bet if'n you had a ride lak this, boy, you be gittin' lotsa poosy!" Herb exclaimed.

"Shore is a poosy car," Andy added. "Ah bet even Herb here cud git poosy inna car like this here."

Herb slowly turned his head toward the back seat, taking obvious offense at the remark, and spoke with a firm voice.

"The *'Erb,* he don't need *no* kinda car to git him poosy. The 'Erb get poosy wheneva he wont it. Good-lookin' poosy too, not lak that toofless old whate poosy you West 'Ginia boys git."

"You thank Ah get me ol' pussy?" Andy asked him. "Ah gits 'em young. Whay, Ah don' do no pussy thet's even legal, wouldn't set right with me. Besides which, you niggers makes too much 'bout heving a mouthful a big whate teeth anaways. Best mouth ta play *ma* horn is a damn good set a gums."

I was glancing in the rearview mirror, and as he said this he grinned expansively; I swear he was showing off his own missing teeth.

"Thet's whate trash talk if I eva heard it," replied Herb. "You mountin boys got no dis-crim-in-ation in poosy. You go stick thet little willy a yo's in any ol' goat if ya git the chance. Now, the 'Erb, he gits onliest the bes'-lookin' poosy. The 'Erb, he a *de*-scrim-in-ate-in' man. Tha's what I bin tryin' to teach the boy heah, you got to de-scrim-in-ate."

"I ain't never met no nigger that de-scrimulates," exclaimed Andy. "Screw a light socket if'n it ain't turned on. Fuck lak rabbits, neva care what goes in or what comes outta thet pussy."

"Whate trash," Herb called out to the road ahead.

"Nigger," Andy yelled at his window.

This was getting serious.

"One mo' *nigger*," Herb yelled out, "and this nigger gonna beat that last toof outta yo' mouf, you nasty ol' cracker!"

"OK, that's enough," I yelled out. "I don't need to hear any more slanders thrown around by either one of you!"

Andy broke the ten seconds of dead silence that followed. "I ain't throwin' nothin' at Herb. Ah don' know what's a 'salander' is, but Ah wasn't throwin' one, Ah jest called him a nigger."

I shook my head, trying to clear my thoughts, when Herb spoke up in a firm and thoughtful voice:

"Sayin' *nigger's easy*. People don' get what *nigger is*. *Nigger's* was what slaves was called inna old days. *Nigger* a nasty low-down thievin' black man nowadays. Ever' way, it a nasty low-down thang ta say to a Negro man if'n you whate. If a man's got prade, he not gonna take it when he called a nigger. Ah ain't no man's slave, I ain't no thief, Ah'm a black man what's got prade. Onliest man call a man a nigger is anotha black man, tha's all."

"That makes no sense," I said. "It's a vicious slur, and you don't say it at *all*. You're telling me it's OK if Speed or the Roach says it to you?"

"Tha's raght, but he got to says it the raght way. If he don't, he gets a whoopin'."

"What's the right way?"

"You got to be black. You ain't no black man so you ain't eva gonna know. No one else in this here car been turned down at no mo-tel fo' a room, nor had ta use no black bafroom, nor gits called no nigger an' hit with a bat till he knocked out, only the 'Erb. Not this rich white boy here nor this ol' foul-mouth whate cracker in the back seat. Lake ta send both you down south lak a black man; see how you two gets along down where I come from. Young white boys got priv-ledge, old whate crackers got priv-ledge, us black folks don't got no priv-ledge."

Andy listened intently but struggled to come up with the right comment. A few minutes passed before he mumbled out the side window; "If'n you ain't no nigger, then I ain't no whate trash. We is what we is, Herbert. Ma lafe ain't been no rose bed. We all of us need priv-ledge."

I wasn't completely naïve. I watched television and saw the budding civil rights movement displayed all over the small screen at home. It seemed, though, so far away. It was on film. There was a reporter speaking from a place called Alabama that to me might as well have been Hong Kong. Martin Luther King never came to Fullerton to speak. We never had a civil rights march downtown. Even if we had, no one would have shown up but white people; they were the only ones who lived there.

It took a good long while for all of this to soak in. I could tell Herb felt badly for scolding us, but hell; we deserved it. It was Herb's way, however, to throw in an abject lesson on pride in order to change the subject again to his favorite topic.

"Ah had me a date one naght," he reminisced, "purtiest girl I eva did know. She was purty, but uppity too. Good lookin' sometames means they don' thank raght. She tol' me, 'Look, mistah, ah don' go to bed with *no one* on the fust date.' Wail, Ah just look her raght in the ayes and says, 'Sugar, Ah ain't *no one*, Ah, is *the 'Erb*'."

I looked in the mirror; Andy was puzzled. "Wail, did ya get pussy or not?" he asked.

"Course Ah did. Ah is *the 'Erb*, "Erb *always* gets the poosy."

That declarative statement hushed the car and allowed me a moment to reflect on something that had never occurred to me due to my teenage naïveté. These two men were alike in many ways, yet culturally there was a vast chasm of experience dividing them. It also crossed my mind that in some ways I was more mature than either of them and it was important to our group chemistry I play the part of the chief, the boss, and, in many cases, the referee. Part of the daily patter I had to listen to was a continual one-upmanship: who was strongest, who won the most on the ponies, who could eat the most, and, most importantly, who had the most success with women. It took me just a few weeks to realize that everything they said was greatly exaggerated. I came to find out they were really faithful family men who merely talked a great game.

There was, however, a downside to all of my contemplation. I neglected to pay attention to the speed of the car, the surrounding traffic, and, most importantly, the amount of rain bouncing off my windshield.

"Stoplaght!" Herb yelled out.

I awoke from my thoughts and found myself in a dicey situation. We were about to cross Imperial Highway just a few miles from our destination, and I was driving too fast. It was a major intersection, heavily trafficked at all times. The difficulty I faced was one every driver faces at times: the light had just turned yellow and I wasn't to the intersection yet. I noticed heavy traffic on both sides of Imperial highway waiting anxiously for the intersection to clear and the light to turn green. I made my decision, I couldn't make it in time; I hit the brakes, hard.

If it hadn't been raining, if the brakes worked well, if I hadn't been going so fast, if pigs could fly, everything would have been just fine. Unfortunately, none of those things happened, and the fun began.

The brakes, being 1966 shitty to begin with, were now soaking wet. This meant that each one of the four would fade, grab, and squeal in whichever way it chose. They chose, in this case, to lock up on the front left side and fade on the right. We lost no speed at all as the rear tires made a hard right turn, putting us into a first-class spin.

The next thing I knew, passing before my eyes was the entire intersection in a rotating 360-degree panoramic view. The stoplight had long ago turned green for oncoming traffic, and at around 270 degrees I was looking into the front windshield of a Ford pickup truck whose driver smartly slammed on his brakes just in time. I can still see his face as we made eye contact.

"I have no control over what is going to happen here," my eyes said to him.

His said, "What the fuck are you doing asshole?

Some moments either happen in slow motion, or your mind just rewinds them that way. I looked to my right and saw Herb's eyes bulging out as if he had been electrocuted; his normally full lips were wire thin and stuck to the outer parts of his teeth, which were now in full bloom.

I glanced in the mirror. I had nothing else to do right then, being totally out of control and all, so I looked for Andy. His face was nowhere in sight, but I could see the hump of his back. He had done what came naturally; he had dived onto the floor.

We spun not once, but twice. A professional driver could have straightened us out by reversing the direction of the steering wheel, but I wasn't a professional driver. The good Lord, however, was a professional savior. Through all the spinning, honking, sliding, and cursing in the pouring rain we wound up on the other side of the intersection, heading the right way, traveling at about the same speed at which we'd entered. I nonchalantly eased my foot back on the gas and, incredibly, we continued on unscathed.

Another long, uncomfortable silence ensued, during which I was trying to act as if this happened all the time.

"Sheeeeeeeeeeeeeeiiiiit," Herb hissed out. It was almost as good as one of Speed's, except that it came out in more of a ten-year-old girl's voice.

"Pull over raght hare," Andy ordered me.

I did not respond; I simply pulled over where he indicated, into the parking lot of a seedy strip center perched alongside the road and parked the car next to a grimy glass storefront with a flashing "Brew 102" neon sign in it. Andy got out of the car and disappeared through a dark tinted glass door that was peppered with Winston, Pall Mall, and Lucky Strike stickers. I was left with Herb, and another awkward silence.

"Wail, boy," he said, "if'n you dadn't know how ta drave befo', you does now. You got ta know somethin'; a young man only gets so many lives. Boy, you jes use one up!"

"Sorry, Herb, the brakes grabbed, and I *was* going too fast."

"My chile jes be glad the 'Erb comin' home tonight," he said more to himself than to me. "Ah thank Ah give her a good huggin'."

The back door opened and Andy scuttled back into the car with a paper bag under one arm and a racing sheet under the other. He settled in and eased the brown twisted paper on the top of the bag down just below the neck of the bottle. He broke the seal on the bottle cap, opened it, and took a long slow swig. Andy then handed the bottle-in-bag forward, in Herb's direction.

"Old Crow," he proclaimed. "Es real good. They keep it on ice in the back room. Ah thank you maght wont a taste."

Herb took the brown bag and looked at it longingly.

"You know, gennemen," he said, "Ah don't drank hard liqa. This, howseva, maght be a special o-ccasion." He looked me right in the eye and took a nice big swallow, never taking those eyes off me. He did not need to say the words; the look was enough, and it told me with certainty: *You caused me to drink this.*

With the same gaze, he pushed the bag straight at me. I took it, drank a hearty swig, tried not to choke, and passed it back to Andy. Andy looked at me, smiled large with those neglected teeth of his, and said, "Old Crow, boss. *Smoooooooth.*"

Chapter Eighteen

THE PARTY

I was staring out the second-story window of the old red brick building they called St. James High School. My right hand supported my head as it hovered over the elbow that rested in the middle of my desk. Eyes wide open; I was fast asleep. This extraordinary ability served me well throughout high school, as my need for sleep seemed to far exceed the amount I was able to actually get. My finest naps occurred in algebra when Father Walsh, who often forgot that there were students in the room while scratching up the blackboard, would turn his back to us for an entire hour, and in Spanish, the class in which I was currently dozing.

Father O'Brien, unfortunately, caught something in my blank gaze that was amiss. A perfectly timed judo chop to the forearm caused my head to drop straight down, driving my chin into the hard pine surface of the desk.

"'R' ya sleepin' ag'in, Mr. Roilly?" he asked as he rolled his eyes up at the cheap drop ceiling tiles. "Yer can't fool me now, pays attention or ya'll get the back o' me hand next."

I could feel blood dripping from my mouth just then, the result of having bitten my tongue when chin hit wood. The only good news was that Jack had thrown a giant soggy spit wad at me to wake me up, and, by virtue of my head dropping, the wad had spun past me and hit "Big"

Mike Yanko in the side of his face. Some of the spittle splashed on my forehead as the giant wad exploded on Big Mike's massive cheekbone.

Mike glared, Jack shriveled. There would be consequences.

After class Jack tried in vain to hide out, but Big Mike found him crouching backward in the janitor's closet just after the lunch bell rang. Mike, having figured out Jack's favorite hiding place, grabbed a handful of his hair and spun his head around to face him.

"Party Saturday night, asshole," he growled. "Have your buddy get the stuff."

Jack could not believe his good fortune. Instead of getting the shit beaten out of him, he had been given a formal invitation to a party!

Big Mike lived up to his name: almost three hundred pounds, he was the all-state, all-muscle, shaved headed left tackle for the St. James football squad, which was considered one of the best teams in the state. I never saw him smile unless he had something particularly nasty to say. Jack, of course, was one of his favorite targets. Ruggedly handsome despite his taciturn personality, he was much sought after by the ladies who attended Marywood Girls' Catholic High School across town.

Jack and I occasionally had a free weekend night when we were not too tired from working to go out. Usually we cruised the local Bob's Big Boy parking lot on Whittier Boulevard, but once in a great while we were invited to a high school party. The principal spot for these get-togethers was a tiny guesthouse behind a decrepit old home on South Broadway in Anaheim that some seniors had rented for the sole purpose of having a place to go to drink, smoke, and meet girls. Jack and I had no redeeming qualities that allowed us to receive an invitation to one of the big Saturday-night orgies at the old house except for one thing: we had access to liquor.

The "buddy" Big Mike had spoken of was Herb. As none of us were of legal age to buy liquor, we had to find a "sponsor" to do so for us. Jack and I had made a deal with Herb that on those nights we went to a party Herb would buy us liquor in exchange for some groceries he could take home to his family. The three of us would drive down to the local Lucky supermarket and go shopping together. Bread, vodka, pinto beans, gin, milk, beer, and so on. Upon the cashier's ringing it all up, I would hand the cash to Herb, who would then hand it to the cashier. Without fail Herb gave us his speech before parting ways: "Ah dasn't care what them others do, but you boys don' be drinking thet ha'd liqa. You kin has some beah, if ya don' drink too much. Liqa is a bad thang, you boys stick to beah an' poosy, an you be awright."

That Saturday night the party was rumored to be a great one. The football team had just won a big game and there was going to be a celebration at the party house. Herb gladly complied with our request for a beverage purchase, so Jack, Herb, and I set out to get the goods.

Outside the market, Herb, out of character, dispensed with his usual sermon. "What you boys got goin' tonight?" he asked.

"It's gonna be a righteous time at the party pad," replied Jack. "Fat fink be there, but I'm not bummed out, lotsa kaak everywhere man."

"We're going to a school party that's supposed to be a good one, football players, but lots of girls too," I translated.

"Kin Ah go?" asked Herb.

The comment surprised me, but my reply had to be; "Sure. You really want to come? It's just a bunch of teenagers."

"Ah wants ta see you boys' frens. Ah neva bin to a white boys' pa-tee."

"Great, only Herb, these aren't really our friends, we just go to school with them."

"I unnerstan', don' worry. 'Erb know how to bee-have at a par-tee, Ah's a young man too, time ago course."

Herb followed us to the party in his car, but we all walked in together.

The three of us definitely looked out of place. We all had our work shirts on, but Jack and I had tucked our shirttails in and spit back our hair in deference to the formality of the occasion. Herb's shirttail flopped outside his baggy pants and there was dried polish spattered all over him.

The three of us held cheap grocery boxes inside of which were liquor bottles of assorted types. I opened the door with my foot and as we three entered the room a mass of teenagers turned, and in unison stopped talking. They stared at us for a good long time; someone interrupted the music. Was it the way we looked, or the liquor in our arms that had spun the spell on the crowd?

I broke the silence.

"Liquor's here, buy it in the kitchen," I yelled out.

We set up shop in the tiny kitchen of the old house. I was the greeter, Jack was the cashier, and Herb was the honored guest. As the thirsty boys came in one by one to make their purchases, I made a formal introduction of Herb to each one.

"This is my business partner, Herb Jackson," I would say.

"Pleased to meet you, Mr. ___," Herb said in his finest Louisiana drawl. He then stuck out that big paint-stained hand and offered it in a sign of friendship. Most of the kids hesitated to shake that hand. They all had to think about it, but finally gave in. Was it the size of his hand? The paint residue splattered on it? Or was it that he was black? I couldn't say for sure, but they did shake his hand. The one exception was big Mike Yanko. Big Mike walked in the room and stared straight at Herb with a typical Big Mike scowl on his face.

"Gimme a bottle of vodka, asshole," he said to Jack as he stared at Herb.

"Hi, Mike," I intervened. "This is Herb Jackson, my business partner. Herb, this is Big Mike Yanko."

Herb completely overlooked the asshole comment, stuck out his hand, and gave Big Mike his million-dollar smile.

"Pleased to meet you, Mr. Mike. Ana fren of the Chief here and Mr. Jack is a fren o' mane."

Big Mike ignored both Herb's smile and his outstretched hand. He turned to Jack, shoved a five-dollar bill in his hand, and grabbed the bottle he was holding.

"Thanks, asshole," was all he said. He turned and walked away.

Herb was troubled, and he looked to me for help. "He not a very frenly man, is he? He got somethin' 'gainst me? Maybe the 'Erb ought not be here."

"No, no, Herb," I replied. "It's just his way. He treats everyone the same, he's just a nasty dude. Because he's a big guy, he can get away with it."

"I tell you Chief, if this was not yo' pa-tee, and if he was an olda man, Ah woulda kicked his fat whate ass all over this litta house raght in front a his frens fo' what he said to Mista Jack heah. Ain't *no* reason to treat a man with no re-spect lak thet."

"Don't worry, Herb, he's just kiddin' around," Jack responded. "He does the same thing to all the dudes at school. I just ignore him; he's got nothin' to do with Stevie and me. Keep your cool, man, there are dickheads in life, and that's the way it will always be man."

Herb was shuffling, ill at ease. We finished our liquor sales while holding back a couple of quarts of beer for ourselves, and I suggested we retreat into the living room where all the activity was taking place.

"You boys go ahead," Herb said to us. "The 'Erb is done worn out, Ah thank Ah need to go home."

We thanked him and said we understood, but a part of me felt bad about putting him in such an uncomfortable position. I'd really wanted him to have a good time, but I'd also selfishly wanted to show him off as a novelty to everyone. I was guilty afterward as I wasn't sure whether I'd done it out of friendship or just wanting to make an impression on my classmates.

Herb's departure did not affect Jack; he wanted to party.

"Let's go mingle, bitch," he said. "There is an abundance of kaak in the big room."

The house was very small. It had a tiny kitchen, one little bedroom, and a decent-size living room strewn with various pieces of cast-off furniture that had been donated, borrowed, or stolen over time. Jack and I tried to look cool as we sauntered in to the beat of the Doors' "Light My Fire."

We took seats next to each other in two avocado-green beanbag chairs stuck in the far corner of the room. Sipping on our quart bottles of Coors beer, we fantasized that we might have a chance with some of the pretty girls who were all busy chatting with the football players.

Across the room, sitting on a couch, were Big Mike and his troupe of best-friend football players. There was Jimmy Nesbeth, another huge lineman, along with Brady Jameson, an all-state linebacker. Mike never lowered himself to hang out with halfbacks or quarterbacks; all his close friends seemed to weigh over 250 pounds.

Each of them had a girlfriend; Mike's was his steady girl Linda Sorenson, a cheerleader, of course, and very cute. She was somewhat petite, weighing about the same as Mike's right arm.

Jack and I were actually having a good time in our own little world as we watched the various partygoers attempt to place themselves in the most socially strategic positions in the room.

Jack began his traditional running commentary: "Mary Jacobs is slobbering all over Matt Jones man. I thought that greaser Matt was gaga for Ann Henderson, what a skeg she is, dude, but not thinking that way now. Is that bitch Tina goin' to go for the jock, or the nerd over there, man, I can't tell, she's a real skank man."

I listened to his banter in silence; he was truly the Vin Scully of party commentary.

Through the mass of people I would occasionally get a glimpse past an arm or a leg of Big Mike sitting on a beat-up purple couch on the other side of the room. He was talking out of the side of his mouth to his friends, but I got the distinct feeling he was staring at us the whole time. Jack continued his commentary oblivious to this, but as he talked, I fixated on Big Mike and wondering what he was up to.

The music stopped. It was time to put a new album on the record player, which in those days took a while. The person in charge of the music had to carefully take the record out of the player without scratching it, replace it in the album cover it had come from, and select a new album. There was a lot of pressure on making the correct music selection depending on the crowd, mood, and time of night, before the person changing the record could reverse the process and place the needle in exactly the right groove on the new record without scratching it.

The gap in the music allowed for more animated conversation, and to my dismay, Big Mike took full advantage of it.

"Hey prick and asshole," he called out, looking directly at us both. "What made you think you could bring a *nigger* in here? *We* decide who gets invited in here, not you. The only reason you two dickheads are here is because you brought the booze."

The room turned silent waiting for our reply. They all knew Herb was *my* acquaintance, so they expected a reply from me. Fear wrapped its muscular arms around my very flexible backbone. What was the right thing to do, to say?

"It's OK, Mike, he's not my friend, he just helped buy the booze. We don't need to have him here anymore if you don't want."

My heart sank; I felt like shit. Some of the crowd, especially the girls, looked down in shame for me. I knew, they knew, that I had given up my friend Herb to save my skin.

Jack, however, had not heard a word I said.

"That '*nigger*' is a friend of ours man," he screamed as he struggled to get up and out of the beanbag chair. "He bought all this liquor you assholes are drinkin' an' you don't want him here?"

Jack wasn't thinking about what he was saying, or whom he was talking to. He occasionally flipped out like this when something, or someone, put him over the edge. Usually I calmed him down after a few minutes and he would start to think rationally, but not this time.

"*FUCK YOU,* you fat-ass, fart-brained, rednecked, suck-ass, chickenshit asshole! You call him a *nigger*? Who the *FUCK* do you think you are? That black man can shit on all of you fat-fuck football players and all those slutty girls you're with."

He may have gone just a bit too far.

The crowd again turned silent. Mike and his friends, I'm sure, had never been talked to this way. They were speechless. Mike's face quickly changed color. White became red. He stood up; everyone's eyes now glued on him to see what would happen, and crossed the room.

"You little faggot," he said, "do you know who you're talkin' to?"

He now stood directly in front of Jack and you could really see the difference in size between the two. Mike was six foot six and weighed three hundred pounds. Jack was about five foot five and weighed a skinny 125 pounds.

Mike picked him up with one hand by the collar of his Clown Burger shirt and lifted him up like an empty can of beer. "I am gonna *FUCK* you up, faggot," he snarled.

Jack flailed his arms and legs around to no avail. It was as though Mike held a fly between his fingertips.

I jumped up out of my chair not having any idea what to do, but knowing someone had to stop the slaughter that was going to take place.

"Put him down, Mike, he's half your size."

"Fuck you, jack-off," he told me. "No one talks to me that way."

And with that he dropped Jack like a sack of potatoes back down on his feet while simultaneously winding up his huge right arm and taking dead aim at Jack's face. Fortunately for Jack, he was savvy enough to do the right thing: he ducked. Unfortunately for me, I was standing next to him, and when he ducked Mike's fist bounced off the top of his head and hit me flush against the side of my nose.

I went down fast. Mike was still raging mad, as I wasn't his principal target. He grabbed at Jack, who was now bobbing and weaving like a miniature Muhammad Ali trying to avoid Mike's gigantic fists. My nose bled profusely and my head throbbed as I sat on the floor. I knew the worst was yet to come as Jack was still darting around but Mike was slowly backing him into a corner. Groggily, I stood up. I could think of only one thing to do.

"Jack, *rule five*," I screamed through the blood.

Jack gave me a quick glance, and I saw a glimmer of recognition in it. He ducked way down in front of Mike, then jumped straight up in the air. This took Big Mike by surprise and he looked at Jack in wonderment. Jack then reared back and kicked big Mike right in the gonads as hard as he possibly could.

Mike's face changed color once again, from red to purple this time, not from anger, but from pain. He wanted to say something, but he could not. Everyone knew he would do anything to kill both Jack and me but, alas, he could not. To his credit, he didn't go down, he simply bent over, grabbed his crotch, and gasped for air.

The crowd was stunned. His friends could easily have beaten the living shit out of both of us if they'd had their wits about them, but they were all in shock. I looked at Jack, he looked at me, and we both executed the second part of rule five: We ran. We ran out of there as if our lives depended on it, and they did.

The next day I showed up for work with one hell of a broken nose. Herb was concerned and wanted to know what had happened. I was embarrassed and did not want to tell him the truth about that night, so I told him I'd gotten into a fight with a football player over a girl. I also told him I'd used rule five but, unfortunately, it was too late. I could tell he wasn't sure I had told him the truth. He knew me well enough to know I would never get in a fight over a girl, let alone with a football player; I was too smart for that. He was, however, willing to let it go.

"Waal, only one cure for that nose, boy," he said. "Sit down there in that chair."

I sat down in my office chair and Herb stood behind me.

"I got ta tell you," he warned, "this gonna hurt, boy, but you too purty to go along with a broken nose rest a yo' lafe."

With that he placed the ham of his hand on one side of my nose and grabbed the side of my head with his other hand. Simultaneously twisting with one hand and pushing with the other, he put my nose back in place.

When I woke up, he was smiling at me.

"Ain't feel too good now, but yo' sho do look betta, boy."

I was in pain, but it wasn't so much my nose. I failed to stand up for Herb, my friend, and there was no way to go back in time and change what had happened. I was a coward, I'd let a bigoted bully push me around, and I was wondering where I really stood with Herb, not only with our friendship, but also with his being black and my being white. It is a discussion I still have with myself, and will for the rest of my life.

Chapter Nineteen

OH, OH, DOMINOES

We were closing in on Christmas, and loneliness was setting in. My brother had been deployed to Germany and would not be home, my father was working all the time and kind of ignored the holidays anyway, and my mother was ensconced in her room leaving me very much on my own. Christmas vacation for me was just another opportunity to work all day long instead of going to school.

Herb and Andy sensed my seclusion and began to include me in a few more extracurricular activities. By the end of the previous summer, Herb had established an event that took place every Friday evening. As with many work-related customs, I had nothing to do with its creation; it just seemed to happen on its own.

Friday afternoons we knocked off early. If cars needed to be delivered, we returned them in time so we could be back at the shop by about four o'clock. Around that time, give or take a half hour, a small, select group of men gathered to play dominoes.

Herb began by clearing off the old wooden desk in my office by carefully stacking my unpaid bills and invoices in the large bottom drawer I left empty for just such occasions. The three paint-flaked metal office chairs were then circled around the desk along with one antique wooden chair brought in from the shop that Speed used to drink his coffee on every morning. The round, black metal light fixture hanging in the middle of the room was turned on, and the old square cardboard box that contained the dominoes was placed in the center of the desk.

Unwritten Rules of Herb's Domino Game

1) *No alcoholic beverages*: At least not in plain sight. (The Roach always carried a flask in his inside jacket pocket so that was taken for granted.) Cream and sugar mixed with coffee was the favored beverage. For safety's sake, no drinks were allowed on the table. (See #2) Spectators were, thankfully, excepted from the alcohol rule.

2) *Proper domino handling*: Slapping dominoes down hard on the table OK, but only if it was a good move. The better the move, the harder the slap and the louder the crack. One should be able to close one's eyes and tell by the crack exactly how good the move was. (*Must never* slap so hard as to change the board or knock coffee out of the hands of players.)

3) *Personal insults*: General remarks concerning a player's ability, or exclamations regarding success or failure were allowed. No comments allowed that reflected on an opponent's personal life, mother, family, sex life, etc.

4) *Seating*: Must stay seated except for bathroom or coffee breaks. This rule did not include Herb, who was uniquely allowed to stand or jump up in a physical display of celebration or contempt.

5) *Etiquette*: Sleeves must be rolled up to just below the elbow. (I wasn't sure if this was to keep from knocking over dominoes on the table, or to prevent a stray piece from falling out of a shirtsleeve.)

6) *Playtime*: Friday night was reserved for the family, clubbing, poosy, etc. (Not necessarily in that order.) A strict time limit of a seven p.m. ending was observed.

7) *Money*: All bets paid at closure. (I never knew the value of each dot, as it seemed rather secretive. I noted that after every game

the players walked outside and exchanged money; to this day I have no idea how much.)

The Players

Herb

The primary host and senior member of the group, Herb was also the most animated and verbose. An interesting study, he could hit the heights of joy with his expansive smile and infectious laugh or go into a very dark and morose place when losing. He was also, by virtue of being the host, the only player permitted to stand up and dance when winning a game.

Speed

Speed was not only a participant; he also shared the heavy responsibility of co-hosting the event. One of the less vocal players, Speed showed a great depth of experience playing the game and excellent hand-eye coordination when it came to slapping down dominoes. His timing was impeccable. Never coming out too soon, he often left the crowd in great anticipation of his next move. He could hover over the table with a domino in his hand for what seemed like hours, waiting until the perfect moment to spring the fateful playing piece on his audience.

Jimmy the Grease

We called Jimmy "the Grease" because he worked for my cousin, Frank Monning, over at Monning Automotive, as a line mechanic. By Friday night his light gray uniform had so much grease on it you couldn't tell where his shirt stopped and his dark, weathered face began. He was short, stout, and bald, with a wispy gray moustache. He looked about thirty or so, but then, who could really tell? Jimmy came over and worked on all our personal cars on his weekends off. I paid him cash to work on my car; I think he might have been paying off gambling debts to the Roach by working on his.

Herb had strict rules for Jimmy. He made him soak his hands in paint thinner and wash them with mechanic's soap before every game. He then rolled up Jimmy's sleeves and placed a towel on his chair for maximum sanitation. Jimmy was a fine player, but a man of few words. He had only two familiar sayings: "Mamma doocie!" (A move in his favor) and "Shiiit fire." (A move that went against him)

The Roach

This was always a mystery to me. I think Herb invited the Roach to play in order to keep himself in his good graces. I assumed everyone's gambling debts were paid up by game time, although it seemed like equestrian wagers were kept completely separate from domino bets. A couple of times, however, the game was canceled as Herb was "delivering cars." (Translation being; he owed the Roach more than was palatable to either of them at the time.)

The Roach always dressed impeccably. His shoes were shined, and he wore a perfectly laundered shirt set off by one of his favorite bolo ties. He was in distinct contrast to the other dusty and dirty workmen at the table. He never cracked a smile, whether winning or losing, but then again, it would have been hard to do with that huge two-dollar cigar sticking out of his mouth. The only saying I ever heard him exclaim during these games was *motherfucker*. If he was winning, it was an animated, uplifting "Motha-*FUCKA*!" If losing, a despondent "*MOTHA*-fucka."

The Spectators

Andy Calhoun - Steven Reilly

We were never invited to play, but then again, we never really felt like joining in. I'm not sure if the domino games were only meant for black players, or we didn't have enough experience, or we weren't properly versed in the rules. Dominoes are simple to play, but Herb's etiquette rules made it much more complicated. Regardless, we were definitely outsiders. No one ever invited us to watch, and I don't know how the practice started other than one Friday afternoon I got back to the shop late and the domino game was well underway. Andy was sitting in a corner on a three-legged stool he'd brought from home, and he was watching the game unfold, as one would study a tennis match. I stuck my head in the door of the office to see what was up. The room reeked of cigar smoke, axle grease, and paint thinner. Andy was the only one to take note of me.

"Pull up a cha'r, boss," Andy said, nodding toward the shop.

I rummaged around and found an empty paint thinner can that was about the right height and brought it inside. I discreetly placed it next to Andy, sat down, and tried to figure out how the game was played.

Looking at Andy's feet, I spotted a plastic paint carton cut in half and filled with ice. Lying in the ice was a pint of Old Crow.

"How 'bout a nip, boss?" he asked me.

I eased the bottle out of its frigid bed, twisted the cap off, and took a nice long pull off the nasty liquid. I looked at Andy. The whiskey warmed my belly; his camaraderie warmed my soul.

I passed the ice-cold bottle back to Andy.

"Smoooooth," I drawled out.

The match was on. Andy and I kept silent as it unfolded. We sipped our whiskey and noted every move.

The Match

Herb's turn:

SLAP-CRACK! The domino is down.

Herb: "Weep, you men, weep! Yas-*sir*. The *'Erb* is *hot* tanaght."
Speed: "Sheeeeeeeeeeiiiiit."
Roach: "MOTHA-fucka."
Grease: "Shiit-fire!!!"

Speed's turn:

Herb: "Speed, you gonna *play* that piece or you gonna *eat* it? Ah got to get home tanaght sometame. Cain't play, you pick from the bone-ya'd, but please, Lordee, *play somethin'!*"

Speed: "Sheeeeeeeeeiiiit," As he holds the domino high in the air where no one can see it.

Roach: "Play that piece, you mothafucka."

Grease: "Momma doocie! You old son-bitch, play o' pass yo' turn."

Speed: After twirling his arm as if he is going to slam the piece down he then delicately places the piece on the edge of the table and slides it slowly into place. "Hee hee hee! Sheeeeeeeeiiiit."

Roach: "MOTHA-fucka."

Grease: "Shiiit fire."

Herb: "You a *beast*, you ol' Speed, but you forget you playin' *the 'Erb*."

The Roach's turn:

With the panache of a most sophisticated player, he coolly flips a piece onto the table.

Roach: "Take that Motha-FUCKA!"

The table goes quiet.

Speed: Dejectedly, he stirs his coffee then spoons a slow bite of it into his mouth.

Grease: "Shiiit fire."

Herb: "Sheeiiit! Where that come from? Das a lucky damn bone, that is. Ah be ma momma's uncle, man cain't find no kinda luck lak that, ain't fair, no way, my momma done tol' me ain't nothin' betta than blind damn dumb luck, don' trus' no man play dominoes (mumble-mumble-mumble)."

Roach: "Count 'em up, boys, ah got three women waitin' tonight. Tha's a lot of pussy to keep waitin', pay up, now, boys, they gonna want some drinks, an' I do need you-all's money to buy 'em with."

More times than not, the Roach seemed to win. Maybe it was because gambling was his business and he knew how to beat these rubes, or maybe Herb let him win to stay on his good side. Either way, I could count on the losers to pull some cash out of their pockets in the parking lot to pay him off.

"Good game," Andy said as things broke up. "Roach wins ag'in, he's lucky, or good, maybe both."

"He may be lucky," I replied, "but he sure ain't good. That guy brings a bad aura in here with him, Andy, I don't like him coming around here."

"Don' rightly know," he replied, "'bout his 'air-a,' boss, but ya raght 'bout his bein' bad.

Say, boss, fergit about that Roach, what you doin' Sataday naght? We havin' a faml'y get-tagetha fo' Christmas and it be nace if'n you could come on over. The whole family will be there, Granny and the wife are cookin' up a storm. I might even break out the ol' fiddle. Come on by about six, we'd be proud to hev ya."

I waited a second or two in order not to seem too anxious. "That sounds great Andy, thanks, I'd love to come. Can I bring anything?"

"No, we ain't much fer gifts neither, jes bring yer own self an' be hongry. We'll have ourselves a hoot."

We shared the last sip of the Old Crow and as I drove home that night I tried to imagine what a West 'Ginia Christmas would be like.

Chapter Twenty

CHRISTMAS AT THE CALHOUNS'

I knew the area well. It was the northeast corner of town, relegated to multifamily housing. Young people just starting out, new arrivals in town, the small but growing Hispanic community, and just plain poor folks wound up living there. I remember being told as a child never to ride my bike anywhere near that particular neighborhood. Most of the apartments were fairly shabby and not very well maintained by the slumlords who squeezed every penny out of the investments other people called homes.

The Calhoun house provided welcome relief from the rest of the dismal neighborhood. Andy and his family lived in the front unit of a large, brown, single-story duplex sandwiched between two faded, red-and-white, two-story apartment complexes. It was freshly painted and had a neat little grass lawn in the front. A randomly colored string of Christmas lights hung lazily across the roofline. As I walked up the old cracked sidewalk I was greeted by a homemade Christmas wreath centered on the front door that was made of blue spruce and adorned with red bows and tiny pinecones. I hesitated before I rang the doorbell, my awkwardness holding me back, but then I gave in.

Andy, thank God, answered the door, and upon recognizing me he grinned a big holiday smile. His thinning hair was neatly Brylcreemed back, he was oddly clean-shaven, and I clearly smelled the pungent odor of Old Crow and cheap aftershave on him. A clean Reilly Detail work shirt was tucked into his over starched denim jeans. The uniform company had thrown in embroidery that week for free, and I think he was particularly proud of the *Andy—Reilly Detail* in script just above his shirt pocket.

"Waill, come on in, boss," he called out as he pumped my hand. "Ever'one's heah, let me show you 'round."

As I walked into the room, a visual menagerie assaulted me along with the cacophony of a big family gathering. There was the distinct smell of warm gingerbread and pumpkin pie wafting through the air as we began our tour. I tried, as we walked, to locate the origin of the various sounds that were emanating from throughout the room. An old record player that sat on a well-worn cherry sofa table was playing Gene Autry's Christmas album as a backdrop. There was an upright piano in the back of the big family room that someone was plinking away on, it might have been "We Three Kings," but I wasn't quite sure. The balance of the din came from the various conversations taking place and voices rising to be heard over one another.

Moving to the right and through the room, we greeted a group of five teenagers sitting on a large overstuffed faded yellow sofa. Randy and Sandy sat on one end, hitting each other in the arm to see who would yell out in pain first. Jamey was fast asleep in the middle, and the two on the other end I could not identify but were obviously family members of some type. They all had work shirts, blue jeans, and mussed longish hair.

"Hey, boss," Randy said, "this here's my cousins, Sammy and Rob Dickson. They live right here behind us."

I was, that night, able to determine through the power of deduction that the extended Calhoun family had rented both units of the duplex and that they currently housed approximately fifteen to twenty family members in the six available bedrooms. Most, if not all, were in attendance that night, along with various assorted friends and more distant relatives.

Andy grabbed my arm to move me along and, as we went, Andy's wife Elle swooped up to me from out of the crowd and gave me a firm hug with one arm.

"Merry Christmas, Steven," she said warmly. "Glad you come, yer sure welcome here."

The other arm lifted up a big red plastic Solo cup in front of my face.

"Andy's Christmas punch," she offered.

The cup was filled to the top with a bright red liquid. Andy watched me closely when I took my first sip. As I rolled the sweet mixture slowly over my tongue, my sharp teenage palate picked up the distinctive overtones of regional punches: Hawaiian and Delaware, - frozen from cans, not the packaged powder, I could always tell the difference - along with a generous splash of Old Crow bourbon and perhaps just a hint of Sav-On vodka. Andy waited for the verdict; I looked down at the cup and whispered, "smooooth." He reveled in the compliment.

I could see now that it was Granny plunking away at the old piano in the back corner of the room. She had a singing audience of three pretty young girls in gingham dresses surrounding her.

"Tha's some o' my nieces o' there with Granny," Andy told me. "Ma sis an' her husband are in the kitchen whippin' up some goodies. They livin' raght behin' us here. Nace to have fam'ly close by."

I walked over to the piano and waved to Granny. She saw me and looked up from the keyboard.

"Merry Christmas, shithead," she called out. She continued to play without missing a beat.

As a group of family members standing next to me moved on, I was able to see the other side of the room. Sitting in an old-fashioned high-backed rocking chair, quietly talking to a pretty young woman standing in front of him was Herb. Next to him, sitting in folding chairs, were what I thought to be his wife, a young girl sitting on her lap, whom I assumed was his daughter, and Speedy Dave.

"You ain't met Herb's fam'ly, hev ya?" Andy asked me.

I gave him a cockeyed look and did not answer. Not that long ago the two of them were heaving racial slurs and epithets at each other, yet here was Herb, sitting in Andy's front room.

"Nace fam'ly," he said. "Wife's smart as a whip, an' they got a cute lil' girl."

I walked across the room trying to catch Herb's eye. He offered me a warm smile when he spotted me.

"Hey, boy, glad ta see ya," he greeted me.

He squeezed my arm and turned me toward the woman sitting next to him. She was somewhat younger than he; I guessed late twenties or so. She was a pleasant-looking, slim, black woman with short, curly, stylish hair. Her outfit was fairly conservative. She wore a white silk blouse and long wool skirt. Herb was as dapper as I had ever seen him, wearing an open-collared white dress shirt rolled up at the sleeves, black slacks, and matching shoes recently polished. The little girl I guessed to be about three or four years old and looked like her mother in an abbreviated form. She, like her father, was dressed for the party. Her hair was in pigtails and she wore a red dress with knee socks that found tiny black shoes where they ended.

"This here's my wife, Lizzie," he said. "Lizzie, this here's the chief, Steven Reilly."

Herb's wife carefully stood the child on the floor next to her and rose out of the chair. It was hard not to notice her height, as she was taller than Herb. Her hand extended and she surprised me with a firm handshake and a big, beautiful smile.

"Well, it's great to finally meet you, Steven," she said. "Herb has spoken well of you and your little enterprise. This is our daughter, Sarah. She just turned four, and you can see she is pretty excited about Christmas."

"Nice to meet you—Lizzie?" I asked.

"Elizabeth," she replied. "Herb calls me Lizzie."

"Elizabeth," I said, "you have a lovely daughter." I looked around the room. "As you can see, Herb and I work with some real characters."

"The Calhoun's are wonderful people, Steven," she replied, "they've been so nice to us. This is like one of the get-togethers my family used to have back home in Chicago."

The woman seemed very sophisticated, and I was somewhat intimidated by her.

"Lizzie gradu-ated from No'thwestern U-versity," Herb said. "I met her in Chee-ca-go. Fam'ly's all back in Chee-ca-go."

I smiled, but was not sure how to keep the conversation moving along. I turned to Speed, who was sitting down quietly eating his coffee with a spoon.

"Hey, Dave," I called out to him. "Merry Christmas!"

He stood up and smiled, happy to have been recognized. He then held his cup up in the air in an effort to make a toast. We all held our cups up weakly. Herb was drinking coffee and Elizabeth had a Solo cup full of Andy's brew, just like mine.

"Sheeeeiit," he began his toast, "Merry Christmas, ever'one. Mista Steven, has you met ma pretty little niece heah? She brung me to the par-tee. Turn 'round, she raght behind youse."

I had not realized my rudeness in that there had been a young woman talking to Herb and Elizabeth as I walked up. She had since turned away, and begun a conversation with someone else while I met Herb's family. She was now standing behind me.

I turned around, as Speed had instructed me to do, and there she was, inches away from me, smiling; looking right into my eyes. Older than I, but not by much, she was the prettiest girl I had ever seen. She looked nothing like her uncle with the exception of her angular face and dimpled chin. Instead of Dave's coal-black wrinkles, she had smooth coffee-colored skin that was set off by a short, fashionable hairdo. Tall, but not too tall, slim, but not too slim, she wore a button-down linen blouse and a blue wool skirt that made her look like a Ralph Lauren model.

"How do you do; Steven, isn't it? I've heard so much about you," she said. "I'm Stephanie, Dave's niece. My uncle loves working for you. My, you sure are young to own your own business."

I tried to speak, but a drop of Andy's punch was the only thing that found its way out of my mouth. No one had ever trained me for such an occasion; no school could teach me what I needed to now know. I was ill equipped to deal with a beautiful woman my age, and I showed it.

Elizabeth sensed my distress and came to my aid.

"Stephanie is attending Cal State Fullerton College, Steven. She's a second-year communications major, just like I was. Isn't that a coincidence?"

Elizabeth looked at me and widened her eyes as if to say, *say something, stupid!*

I snapped out of it, sort of. "You're learning how to communicate?" was all I could think of to say.

She laughed; Elizabeth just rolled her eyes.

"Not in conversation, apparently," Stephanie replied. "I guess I better stick with writing."

I laughed, because I thought I should.

"Sorry, Stephanie, I can do better. You know, I like to write too, it's kind of a hobby of mine, when I have time, of course."

"My uncle said you were still in school Steven, what college do you go to?"

Moment of truth: I was conflicted, but I had no time to mull over my delicate position. Should I tell her the truth, that I was still in high school, or tell some kind of half-truth that might lead her to believe I was older? At our age, and at that time, a girl's being a few years older and in college would set us miles apart.

I had to tell the truth, only because I knew she would find out one way or the other.

"I'm graduating this spring, I think I'm going to Cal State as an English major, maybe business as a minor."

"Oh," she said, now knowing my age, "I see. Well, I hope you go there, we might get to see each other."

I then realized I had created another uncomfortable pause in the conversation; something, with girls, I was really good at.

She broke the silence: "I hear you and Herb are pretty good friends, Steven."

"Not really," I told her. "He works for me just like Dave and Andy, but I have to keep everything businesslike. It's a business, they're employees, you know what I mean?"

I was showing off, and it backfired. She saw through my silly attempt to appear more mature than I really was. I had to once again deny Herb's friendship to do it.

"I need to go help Elle in the kitchen, Steven, I'll catch up with you later."

She turned and left as quickly as she had appeared. I was sure I had said the wrong thing.

Elizabeth looked at me with a mother's eyes. "What a nice girl," she said. "Pretty too, don't you think?"

I was staring off in the direction Stephanie had left in.

"She's beautiful," I said to no one in particular. I shook my head and tried to get my wits about me.

"I have a feeling she likes you. You need to follow up on that, Steven."

"Way over my head, Elizabeth. She might make someone a great girlfriend, but I'm afraid it's gonna be the senior captain of the baseball team at Cal State Fullerton."

"Don't sell yourself short, Steven. You two may have more in common than you think. Besides, she seems like the kind of girl that cares more about what's inside you than all that superficial stuff. She seems really grounded, and she's smart. Maybe you meet those kind of girls all the time, but I doubt it."

Elizabeth suddenly jumped up and let out a shriek. Herb had come up behind her and grabbed her by the waist, surprising her.

"Lizzie, what you tellin' the boy here? You been yakking a good lot ova here."

"We were talking about Dave's niece," she replied. "I think Steven is a bit sweet on her."

"Waill now," he said, "I ain't blame ya, boy. She is a fane young girl. If I wasn't in such wunnerful love with this here woman, the 'Erb would be after that one fo' sho'."

Elizabeth punched him hard enough in the arm to make him flinch. "Go get Sarah," she said to him. "Let's all go sing some Christmas carols with Granny."

Granny was still at the piano playing her traditional Christmas music. She played precisely, but with little feeling, like someone who had taken lessons only as a child.

We gathered around the old piano and everyone then parted to let Andy through. He had a black, weathered, old violin case under his arm. He placed the case on the piano top and gently opened it up. Out came one of the finest-looking violins I had ever seen. The antique burled wood was polished so finely it reflected the red lights on the Christmas tree like a mirror. Long hairy string ends hung off the tuning screws begging to be trimmed. More than a musical instrument, it was a splendid object of art.

Andy pulled out the bow, closed the case, and then picked up the violin as if it were a newborn baby. He cradled it in his arms and plucked at the strings with his right hand. With the other he deftly adjusted each string with the corresponding turnbuckle until he was completely satisfied with the resulting sound.

He then positioned the base of the violin under his chin and made an announcement to the assembled crowd. "This hare's ma daddy's fiddle. 'Fore thet, it was my granddaddy's, and 'for thet, his daddy's. It's I-talian. Daddy said a fella called Strad-i-very done made it, but then ag'in, Daddy done tol' some whoppers in his day."

With that, he stood next to Granny who was waiting for her cue; this wasn't the first time they had performed together. Granny began with a flourish, but wound up with the background part of "God Rest Ye Merry Gentlemen" as Andy caressed his fiddle with a stirring rendition. The melody was perfect; you could, however, pick up some West Virginia riffs thrown in for seasoning. The crowd joined in, all of us. Elizabeth, standing next to me, sang in a beautiful high-pitched delicate voice. Speed sounded like a bullfrog on steroids.

One voice, however, stood out above the others. It was a deep rich baritone. I turned to peek at the source: it was Herb.

I never thought about it at work where he sang all the time. He did so almost absentmindedly but it was always background music to work by. Here, though, tonight, I could see and hear the joy he had all bottled up inside him. I think it was his family there with him that opened him up. He could rightfully take pride in them and show them off to Andy, to Speed, and to me. His family and his friends here, he was happy; he was free to be himself.

In the middle of "Jingle Bells," however, I felt a slight tug on my elbow. Turning around, I saw it was Elizabeth motioning me away from the crowd. She had me follow her into the kitchen that was now empty of anyone who could listen in to our conversation. It appeared as if something important was on her mind.

"Steven," she said, "do you know this 'Eddie' character who is supposed to be a friend of Herb's?"

The question made me uneasy, and I wasn't sure how to answer.

"Yeah, sure, he comes around once in a while and plays dominoes. I don't know him very well, he doesn't talk much."

"I'm afraid of him," she replied. "He's got our phone number, and he calls me looking for Herb. Herb says to tell him he's not home, that he's just a lonely guy looking for someone to pal around with. I think there's more to it than that. What do you know about him?"

I felt obligated to both of them, to tell her what I knew, but also to keep Herb's confidence. On the other hand, I didn't have proof, and I wasn't sure of anything concerning the Roach. Most of my thoughts were just opinions; opinions, I figured, I should keep to myself.

"I really don't know what the guy's all about, Elizabeth. His last name is Roché; we call him the Roach. He drives a nice car and is pretty dapper. He comes around looking for Herb once in a while but I don't know anything else. Herb doesn't talk about him."

"You don't think Herb is mixed up in something illegal, do you?"

"Naw, Herb wouldn't do anything like that, maybe he just feels sorry for the guy."

"Something tells me he's not the kind of guy you feel sorry for. I have a bad feeling about this, Steven. You keep an eye on that guy and don't be afraid to ask Herb about him. Herb trusts you, he can talk to you about things I can't."

"I don't know, Elizabeth, I'm just a young kid to him. He keeps a lot of his world away from me. I'm not sure if that's to protect me, or him, but that's just the way it is."

"Well, I think he looks at you as a lot more than just a young kid, or his boss, Steven. You should hear the way he talks about work sometimes. I've never seen him so happy, and that makes me happy. I don't need anything or anyone to get in the way of that. Keep your eye on this Roach guy for me, OK?"

"I will," I told her. "Herb's always there for me when I need him, I'll watch out for him, don't worry."

She didn't look fully convinced as she turned to walk away; she looked back at me once more. "Thanks, Steven. You're a good man."

It was time for me to leave the party after Herb and his family had said their farewells. I tried to find Stephanie to at least say goodbye to her, but she was gone. I was heartbroken, but then again, I was also relieved. I no longer would bear the burden of thinking about her and what might have been. She was out of my league, she probably had a boyfriend, and I had no chance. It was still a crushing defeat. The other girls I met at school dances were young, they were childish, and they had yet to blossom into young women who looked and acted like Stephanie. I needed to forget about her as I had forgotten about all the others I was ever interested in. It was the one thing I was really good at.

Chapter Twenty-One

SAGE ADVICE

It was January 1967. Winter in California meant clear, beautiful days with only an occasional rainstorm to break the balmy monotony. The sun was still setting early, however, and most deliveries ended with a ride home in darkness. Herb preferred to go on these deliveries even though they kept us from getting home at a reasonable hour. Speed told me that the Roach came by every day about five on his regular collection run, so it was no coincidence that Herb wanted to be gone around that time.

I was going to drive a white, "plain-Jane" 1962 Chevy Biscayne two door up to Doug Shultz, while Herb was assigned to pick me up in a car he would drive over from the Volkswagen dealer. Herb looked agitated as he hurried to leave well before me. I inspected the Chevy for any imperfections my father might call me on and jumped in the front seat. I grabbed the armrest to close the door, but it did not budge. I tried again and failed. I looked over at what the obstruction was, and then looked up. A fat-fingered, coal-black hand was wrapped around the top of the window frame, preventing me from closing it.

"Wheah is 'Erb?" I heard the voice bellow. I looked behind me and to the left; it was the Roach.

"He went home, sir," I said. "It's late."

"Ah said, *where is Herb?*" he repeated.

"Mr. Roché," I replied, "I said he's gone home. I don't keep track of him after hours, that's not my job."

"You tell Herb," he said, "that Ah is lookin' for him. Now Ah kin find him, but better for him he comes to me. You got that, boy?"

He had moved his face closer to mine with each word. He was close enough now I could smell his breath: whiskey and cigars, I thought, covered up with a capful of Listerine. I was nervous, scared, but not like Mike Yanko scared. This was different.

"I understand," I choked out. "I'll tell him. When I see him."

He closed the door and walked away. I sat for a few minutes wondering how deep Herb was in to him, and how I'd gotten in the middle of it all.

It was well after sunset by the time Herb and I left the Chevy dealership together. We were tired and anxious to get home. Herb, however, was never too tired to talk. He seemed to always have a deep reservoir of counsel to offer me, and the drive back provided the time for my schooling. I told him about the Roach showing up at the shop, but he refused to talk about him and quickly changed the subject.

"You eva call that nace girl from the par-tee?" he began. "Ah think tha's Speedy's niece. Ah see you lookin' at her. Heh heh heh." He barely moved his lips. He sometimes laughed like this; the way a ventriloquist might laugh with a dummy in his arms.

"Naw," I replied, "she's out of my league, older, good-looking, and smart. I need to find somebody that suits me better, you know, a more average girl."

Herb snapped his head sideways and barked at me, "Ain't no woman out of the 'Erb's league, ain't no women be out o' *yo'* league if you don' want 'em to be. Wassa matta with you, boy? You not *stupid*, is you? That girl lak what she see! She be yo' girl if you want, you just got ta decide if you wont her!"

I had to think through my answer carefully. Herb was a safe place for me; he was the only person in my life I felt comfortable enough with to talk openly and honestly. It wasn't because he didn't criticize me; he did, all the time. It was the way he spoke to me, as if he cared about what I had to say, when it seemed no one else really did.

"Honestly, Herb," I replied, "I don't know how. What would I say, how would I say it? I'm not a charmer like you. It takes a gift of gab, a quick wit, and I don't have it. I'll never see her again."

"You may not see her, but tha's *yo'* choice, boy, not hers. Ya-suh, the 'Erb got the looks, an' the 'Erb talks good, but you smart e-nuff to say what need ta be said, you just got to get the gumption up ta do it. Ya know, boy, you is trapped in some bad *notions*. Them *notions* make no sense. You got to git them *notions* outta yo' head, boy, if'n you wants ta git you a woman."

"OK, say I lose the notions and *get* the gumption. What do I say? I never come up with the right thing, it always comes out wrong and I get embarrassed."

"You tell 'em the truth, boy, an if'n they don' like it, they the ones thet lose, not you. How's 'bout, 'Hey, girl, Ah seen you fine ass at the par-tee, how 'bout you an I go out an talk 'bout me gettin' some that sweet poon-tang tanaght?' Heh, heh, heh."

"Now don' gimme thet look, boy, Ah serious, you tell her you seen her at the par-tee, an' you wanna go out with her! Now, you try it on the 'Erb."

He cocked his head up and looked away like a sullen schoolgirl.

"Hi, Stephanie," I said in my usual drab, monotone voice. "I saw you at the party and thought maybe you and I could go out sometime."

Herb shook his head in disgust. "It ain't jes *what* you say, boy, it *how* you says it. Now you says it the 'Erb way. '*Hey, girl*, I *seen* you at the *par*-tee, an' I *loves* to see you ag'in. Le's us go out sometame. Be *nace* ta get ta know ya. Fra-day naght, pick you up at yo' house.' See, boy, women, they *lak* men that speak up. Nature done tell em that bash-ful ain't what you lookin fo'. Bash-ful man don' watch out and pro-tect her, spoken-up man do. You got to speak up an be a man. Tha's what women lak."

"OK, say I get through and get a date. What do I talk about? I'm not that interesting to most people, let alone some bright college girl."

"Boy, I be tellin' you somethin' you got to learn sometame. Women ain't much different than men that way. You want a woman to lak you; you talk about *her*. You ask 'em what they lak, what they do, what they fam'ly all 'bout. You be interested in them, an' you be in fane shape. Same fo' men, if'n you want to get ahead in this wirl, you be in-ter-ested in other people an' what *they* thinkin'. You gotta stop this feelin' sorry fo' yo'self and thinking only 'bout yo' silly-ass prob-lems an start thinkin' 'bout the people you with."

Anyone else could have said it and I would have just blown it off. I *was* a self-absorbed young man who had never learned the key to good social skills and maybe never would have without a life lesson from someone like Herb. My father was a good salesman, but it was all fake. You could see right through it, and it was partly his superficial attitude toward me that kept us apart. I'd always thought being shy was a virtue. Honesty meant no bullshit, no forced conversation, and no silly questions.

"She'll see right through it," I said. "Dumb questions about her family and school. It would be obvious that I was just trying to chat her up. That's not me, it's not who I am."

"So, you not interested in her?" he replied. "In what she think? What she lak? What kinda wirl she lives in, boy? You ain't shy, you stupid, thet all! You gonna live in a cave somewhere? Look, you gonna get ta know people you got to talk to 'em. Find out wha's goin' on with 'em; *that's* how you make friends, and boy, *that's* how you gonna get you some poosy!"

"OK, I get it. It just doesn't come naturally to me like it does to you that's all. It doesn't feel right, but I'll give it a try."

"You got nothin' to lose, boy, 'cepting maybe a little skin off that skinny little white pecker o' yo's."

"Why is everything about sex with you?" I shot back. "Man, sometimes I wonder if you have any morals at all. The way you talk, all that counts is how many women you take to bed. You're supposed to be a family man and yet you brag to everyone how many women you're with. Maybe we need to talk about your problems Herb, not mine."

He was taken aback by the comment, and I could tell he was hurt.

"My fam'ly is *ma* business, ain't yours, boy. Men talk 'bout poosy alla time, but that don't mean they gittin' it alla time. My poosy days; they over. That don't mean the 'Erb cain't talk 'bout it. Now, you a young man, young man should be talkin' *an' gettin'* poosy. Don' you tell me wha's raght and wha's not, boy. Ah live by the Bible. Bible says somethin' raght, Ah live by it."

"The Bible doesn't say you can screw every woman you want," I told him.

"Now tha's where you mostly wrong, boy. Bible says young men and young women's need to get togetha. God say, 'Go begat, you young men and young women.' Begat means man be-gatting some poosy, see. He says begat here, begat there, you all got to begattin'; begattin' what? *Poooosy*, tha's what! Time for you to begin begattin', boy. Bible say so, God say so, Ah say so. You ain't begattin' if you ain't calling thet gal an' you ain't begattin' if you don' crawl youself outta that shell you in and start talkin' like the 'Erb do to women."

I was trying to reconcile Herb's interpretation of the Bible with the Catholic version I'd learned, and it wasn't working. One of them would eventually win out, and down deep I knew Herb was right, but I was still a product of my childhood. My vision had always been of a shy and pure boy meeting a beautiful, shy, and pure girl, and we would get married without having to say a word to each other. Now I was being told that I had to *work* at getting that girl. I would have to *talk* to her and then somehow figure out how to have sex with her. It seemed, back then, an insurmountable task.

I was naïve about those facts of life; Herb wasn't so sure about the other ones:

"Boy?"

"Yeah, Herb?"

"You know how gittin' poosy woiks, don'tcha?"

"Whatta ya mean, Herb?"

"Youse know. Man cain't turn on the water if'n he don't know how the plumbin' woiks."

"What the hell you talkin' about, Herb?"

"Wail now, a man gonna plant seeds, he got to know how ta use his hoe."

"You talkin' about havin' sex, Herb? Hell, I'm seventeen years old. How do you know I haven't *had* sex? Just 'cause I don't have a girlfriend doesn't mean I never had sex."

"Not sayin' that, boy. Just sayin', once you lower you'self down in that there mine shaft, you got to know where to put that pickax or you ain't gonna get no coal."

"I *know* where the pickax goes, Herb. What made you think I don't anyway?"

"Wail, the 'Erb just wanna make sure little Stevie down there, and big Stevie inna you head, be on the same page, so's to speak. Did yo' daddy eva tell you 'bout coal mining?"

"Quit using those stupid metaphors, will ya! No, my dad never talked about *coal mining*. He never talked to me about anything. My biology teacher, Mr. Quinn, taught us everything we need to know in school, and I probably know more than *you* do about sexual function."

"You neva has poosy yet, has you, boy?"

"OK, OK, no, I haven't, but when I do, it's not gonna be in the back seat of a car behind a sleazy bar somewhere, it's gonna be the right way, and I *will* know what to do."

"Awright, awright, you don't got to be so sen-sitive, boy. 'Erb jest wanna make sure you OK in that de-partment."

"OK, OK, I'm fine down there, let's drop it, Herb, I got it, I got it."

"Nuff said, boy. Jest that—man shoots a game a pool, he jest gotta know how ta use the pool-stick, an which balls ta hit, that's all."

My ego was somewhat bruised by now, and Herb would have gone on forever; I *had* to change the subject. "Herb," I said, "Why do you call me boy?"

He put his hand to his chin and twirled his wispy goatee in thought. "No sah," he replied. "Ah call you chief."

"Only at the shop, when someone's around. Any other time, you call me boy."

"Waill, Ah suppose you kind of a boy to me, Ah's older than you, an a man."

"I don't like it. I may be young, but I'm your boss, and I'm a man, just like you. My dad called you boy once and I saw you bristle, I'm not any different."

"Boy a *slave* term, boy, Ah mean Chief," he corrected himself. "Diff'rent for black than white. No black man wants to be called boy when he's a man. Es *de-gradin'*."

"OK, I get that, only I don't feel any different. Can't I get the same respect?"

He had no pat answer for that; he focused instead on working the clutch and shifting the gears, which he did in a rather clunky manner. Herb hated the stick shifts I loved so much.

"What you want me to call you?" he asked me. "Cain't call you chief alla time."

"My name is Steven. You can call me Steven, Steve, Stevie, or Shithead, just don't call me boy."

He broke out in a big smile.

"You learnin' fast, *Steven*. You got to ask for what you want in lafe. Sometames, you jest maght get it."

Chapter Twenty-Two

SLOW DANCIN'

Two weeks later I was behind the wheel of a magnificent black Cadillac two-door convertible. It was a 1964 Coupe de Ville with a white leather interior that matched the power fold-down top. The car was as big as an ambulance with the power of a fire truck. I'd gotten it from my father. The beast wasn't really his; he just drove home any car he wanted to off of the used car lot every night. I'd begged him to loan me a decent car for this special occasion, and for once, he came through. My old '54 Ford just wasn't up to the task.

We were on our way to the senior dance, not as important as the prom, but definitely a premier event on the social calendar for those who cared about solidifying their relationships for the end-of-the-year parties and dances.

Staring at me in the rearview mirror was Jack, sitting in the back seat. He'd begged me to bring him along, as the generator on his Chevy Corvair had blown up and he had no way to get there. He was playing in the band that night, so we wound up fitting most of his drum set in the cavernous Caddy trunk. His huge bass drum, however, wouldn't fit, and was now sitting next to him in the back seat.

Jack looked particularly weird that night, even for him. Our Dean of Discipline, Father Ryan, had given him a number one head shaving as retribution for having put Ben-Gay, a form of liquid heat used for muscle strains, in the boys' shower's soap dispensers the previous week.

Jack had done it for the benefit of the basketball team, of which Big Mike was a member. It was his payback for the comment about Herb and my broken nose. Father Ryan was more perturbed at Jack for breaking the truce with Big Mike than for the prank itself. After the party and the broken nose incident, someone had ratted to Father Ryan about what happened that night and he had to pull a "Godfather" threat on Big Mike in order to save Jack and me from further bloodshed.

"If anything should happen, Mr. Yanko," Father began as he stood over Big Mike, who was sitting on the punishment stool in the corner of the dean's office, "to Mr. Reilly or to Mr. Brown, for any reason, if they should trip on the sidewalk, or if they were to fall in the shower, any *accident* at all, you, Mr. Yanko, will never, ever, graduate and see a football scholarship, anywhere, anytime, at any college, so help me God."

Due to the head shave, Jack's ears that night looked five times bigger than usual and he reminded me more of Mickey Mouse rather than Mr. Spock. They stuck out prominently beneath the red beret he was wearing in the hope of covering his temporary baldness. He had found a goofy-looking purple jacket at the thrift store and wore this over a white Crow Surfboards T-shirt. I was just hoping that later on he would sit at the back of the stage, hidden by his drum set, where no one could see him.

"Sweet ride, Cosmo," he called out from the back seat. "Many thanks and peaceful resolutions to you, man. Stoked you would bring me to the dance and, I gotta say, fine-looking kaak you got there, kemosabe. I'm thinking I know you, girl. Saw you at Frito's Clubhouse, I think. Play there sometimes when the regular band gets shit-faced and don't show up. Whatta you say? Frito's?"

I looked over at Stephanie; she forced a smile, and I knew then I had made a big mistake. My friendship with Jack was always destined to doom me, and here we all were.

"Nooo, I don't think so," she replied. "I'm not sure what Frito's is, but I've never been there."

"Well, you oughta go. It's a bitchin' place. Only thing is, I'm a young dude, but they still let me drink beer on the breaks. I myself got shit-faced one night and kicked the pedal right through my bass drum. Look here, you can see there's a brand-new skin on it man."

"Jack," I told him, "can you just be quiet until we get there? I'm actually on a date here, and you need to pretend you're invisible back there."

"Oh, sorry, man, I was just di-rectin' traffic here man, you know, fillin' in the gaps in the conversation, so to speak."

I *was* nervous. I had taken Herb's advice and called Stephanie. Dave had filled me in on her background. Her mother, Dave's sister, brought her out to San Francisco from Detroit when she was very young. She'd attended Catholic grammar and high schools there, so at least we had that in common. Cal State Fullerton had given her a full-ride academic scholarship, and that was how she'd ended up in Orange County.

Any sane bachelor would have taken her out for a drink and gotten to know her first, but I wasn't old enough to legally drink and the only other activity that came to mind was the big dance.

I put the top down on the Cadillac, just for effect, and parked in front of the plain-looking student apartment complex where she lived, which was located right across the street from the college. As she opened the door and greeted me with her perfect smile I saw that she was as gorgeous as I remembered. She wore a very stylish, short, black, form-fitting dress, and her hair was up in a fashionable do that someone had spent a lot of time on.

I looked rather dapper myself that night. I wore a thin black tie that hung lazily on a white button-down J. C. Penney short-sleeved shirt. The blue blazer I had taken from my brother's closet set this off nicely, even if it was a size too big for me. I'd pomaded my hair straight back and applied a heavy splash of English Leather cologne. I looked, and smelled, much like every other seventeen-year-old boy at the dance that night.

Alone in the car with her, I was uncomfortable and quiet. Her beauty flummoxed me, and my communication skills were being tested.

I *was* relieved when we picked up Jack; I was sure he would break the silence.

"There it is," Jack screamed out. "Hit it dude."

We were traveling down Olive Street, a road I knew well, on the way to Marywood Girls' Catholic High School where the dance was being held. There was a railroad track that ran right through the middle of town, and up ahead it ran perpendicular to the street we were driving on. The thing about this particular crossing was that it was raised up on a bump in the road a good several feet higher than street level. Normally one would just slow down and roll over the protrusion in the road, but it was somewhat of a tradition to take the bump at speed and see if you could get your car airborne. Not much, just enough to talk about.

The problem confronting me on this particular occasion was that I usually drove Chevrolets, Fords, and Volkswagens over the hump. The Caddy, however, weighed about five tons and must have been about thirty feet long. I pushed lightly on the gas pedal to take the bump as I normally would, but at the last minute I realized the weight could keep us from getting airborne and we might hit it flat, on the underside of the car. My instincts took over: I hit the gas.

I was right: the extra power and speed lifted the mighty mammoth of a car up and over the railroad tracks, shooting us up into the air, where we experienced a brief moment of bliss.

The bliss *was* brief. The Caddy came down on the other side like a building coming down in an earthquake. None of us had seat belts on; nobody wore them back then. The suspension compressed with such force that all four shock absorbers collapsed and the rebound sent all of our heads into the lightly padded roof with a bang. Through great effort I was able to finally slow the deflated tank down and stop the car along the side of the road.

I looked at Stephanie. Her beautiful hair-do was smashed down like a pancake.

"Are you OK," I asked her.

"I think so," she responded coolly. She put her hand to her head and realized what had happened to her hair. "I may need to do some repair work, but I'm not hurt Steven. What the hell was that all about?"

I looked back at Jack to see if he was OK.

"Whooooo yeah!" he yelled out. "Awesome, dude! Radical liftoff!"

I got out of the car, Jack was right behind me. The shocks' being blown out made the car sit just a few inches off the ground, and there was smoke settling in around each tire well. Today they might call the broken Caddy a "lowrider," but at the time it just looked sick. The force had been so hard that it blew off the hubcaps about twenty feet in each direction. Jack and I walked back, looked around, and found the bruised hubcaps strewn alongside the road. We picked them up and threw them in the trunk. I don't know why I was mad at Jack, but I was; it was my fault, I should have known better.

"Wow, dude, hope you don't get in trouble for this. That was crazy, man."

I closed the trunk lid. "Jack," I said, "shut up! If I can get this car moving again, I want you to shut your mouth the rest of the way. I'm trying to make a good impression on this girl, and it's not going real great so far. And give me the two dollars you owe me for the ride, Jack. You're gonna forget later and I want the cash now."

I could tell his feelings were hurt. He pulled out his beat-up old black nylon wallet and opened it up. He looked inside and then snapped it shut quickly.

"Sorry man, I got to divvy up later, I don't got the bread right now."

I grabbed the wallet out of his hand before he could prevent it from happening. I opened it up and pulled out a brand-new hundred-dollar bill I'd caught a glimpse of when he had cracked it open.

"What the fuck is this?" I asked him. "A hundred? You've never seen a hundred-dollar bill in your life! Where'd you get it?"

He looked aghast. "Umm, I got paid, man. I got money, I just ain't got the two bucks I owe ya."

"You didn't just get paid! You've never had a paycheck from the Clown for more than twenty bucks, and I sure didn't give it to you for drivin' cars. Where did you get it, Jack, and why are you lyin' to me?"

"Everything all right, Steven?" It was Stephanie calling out from her window.

"Yeah, sure," I replied. "We're just makin' sure everything's OK. Be right there."

Jack was looking down and kicking a loose pebble with his well-worn brown cloth loafers.

"What's up, Jack? Come clean, now!"

He wouldn't look me in the eye.

"The Roach gave it to me, man."

"What? Why on earth would the Roach give you any money, let alone a hundred dollars? That makes no sense."

"Dude, it's like a *job* man, you know. I'm doin' a *job* for him, that's all."

"A *job*? What kind of job pays a hundred dollars, Jack? You tell me what's goin' on, right now."

"He said it's payment for a job, that's all. He said Herb was in money trouble, and he was worried about him. I'm supposed ta tell him where Herb is, and what time he leaves work each day. He said he's his friend and he wants to protect him. Kinda like a bodyguard, you know man?"

"You really think that's what he wants to do, Jack? Protect him?"

"I don't know *man*. That's what he said. I didn't see no harm. Why shouldn't I believe him?"

"Because he's the Roach, that's why, you *dipshit*! He's the one after Herb for money, and you knew it. You took the money anyway. What else did he say? Tell me now, Jack."

"He said, well, he said to look after you too. Let him know where you both was all the time. I wasn't gonna fink on ya, Stevie, I swear. I just took the money. I was gonna make stuff up and hope he thought it was real. I was gonna tell ya, man, I just didn't get the chance."

"Yeah, right, you were gonna tell me, Jack. You piece of shit! Why would he care about *me* anyway? I don't owe him any money. Herb's doings don't have anything to do with me."

"I don't know, man. He said he was worried about ya both. Herb plays dominoes with the guy, man. He's his friend. He ain't gonna do nothin', man. Quit makin' a big deal outta this. Let's go man."

"It better not be a big deal, Jack. This guy's not Herb's friend, and he's not yours either. You give back that hundred and you tell him it was too hard to keep track of us that we never told you where we were going. You don't want any part of whatever's goin' on. You do it Monday, and if he gives you any grief, you let me know."

He looked down again; I grabbed his chin and pulled it up to my face.

"You understand?"

"Yeah," he said, "I understand."

We got back in the car and I turned to Stephanie.

"Sorry," I told her, "just wanted to make sure the car was safe to drive."

I started the car with a silent prayer I could get us out of there, and it was answered. I had to drive slower and more carefully now. With no shock absorbers the car rode like a buckboard: we could feel every bump in the road. I could tell Stephanie was upset, and rightly so.

"I'm sorry, Stephanie," I apologized. "I'm normally a very good driver. There was just a moment there; Jack got me all worked up. I promise, no more surprises."

"Let's just go to the dance, Steven, carefully, please."

*****

As we walked through the multicolored horseshoe of balloons at the entrance of the Marywood Girls' High School gymnasium, I realized we were out of place. It wasn't Jack; he had left to play with the band. It was me, or should I say, it was Stephanie; then again, it was me, *with* Stephanie. She looked like a movie star, and I looked like the pimply teenager I was. Everyone was staring at us, and I knew the rumors would fly.

There was a tremendous amount of diversity at the Marywood dances, and you could see it as soon as you walked in. The bolder girls wore red sweaters instead of white ones; some daring to wear them wrapped around their shoulders instead of their waists. The skirts they wore were identical except for a bold few who opted for dark brown instead of white; the blouses were all crisp, white, and revealed nothing.

The boys all wore the exact same outfit as mine. I did, however, spot a black blazer in the crowd instead of a blue one, and a few of the guys had made the horrible mistake of wearing a traditional collar instead of a button-down.

Had I known anything other than blond, white-skinned teenagers even existed, I would have looked for, but not found them. The thought that Stephanie was African-American and was sure to stand out at the dance had not occurred to me, or maybe it had subconsciously. I remembered the night we'd taken Herb to the party. I was actually proud, proud of the fact I had a black friend; something no one else I knew could brag of. I'd felt ashamed afterward for treating someone, a friend no less, as a novelty. Tonight I felt a twinge of the same shame, but only in the background of my mind, as, to me, she was first and foremost a beautiful girl whom I was very much attracted to.

I scanned the assembling cliques on either side of me as we walked through the center of the gym turned dance hall. The boys were generally assembled on the left of the main walkway, the girls on the right.

Mary Hemmert's smart girls were the first we saw. Mary was covering her mouth and whispering to Betsy Palmer as we walked by.

Linda Sorenson and the cheerleaders were next; their mouths were wide open with surprise at the sight of us.

On the left I saw Big Mike and the jocks: most of them just stared, except for Big Mike, who mouthed a silent obscenity at me.

The surfers blended into the cool dudes next and I was rewarded with a few thumbs-ups by that group, although there were also a few shaking heads.

I thought I knew what the comments would be:

"Where did he get this girl?" "The guy's a nobody!" "Did he pay her?" "The guy's a dweeb!"

It took me a moment, and then it came to me, what the other ones might be:

"Is she really black?" "He's dating a black girl?"

It is always hard to take a group of people and generalize about them, and I'm sure most of the kids at the dance were good-hearted souls who lacked any overt prejudice against people of color, but it had to be on their minds. I was sure, however, that there were some, like Big Mike, who were downright bigots.

I wondered also as we walked down the line of girls on one side and boys on the other if sex had anything to do with prejudice.

Were men genetically hard-wired to protect the group from outsiders who might look and talk differently? Did the women seek better providers from outside the group and be more open to them? Had we passed these genetic traits on through the ages until they culminated in a room full of preconditioned teenagers?

I could sense the reactions as we walked through though it may have been my own genetic conditioning talking back to me. The boys saw her as black first, the girls thought of her as beautiful first.

Boys: "Reilly is with a black girl. Wow, she is really good-looking."

Girls: "Reilly is with a gorgeous girl. I think she might be black."

This was a girl, however, who showed the other girls something much different than her skin color. Stephanie showed them all what a sophisticated young woman should look like, dress like, and act like. Someone those girls all aspired to be someday.

I looked at Stephanie and tried to imagine what was going through her mind. From the first time I had met her she'd given no thought to her looks, our age gap, or our racial differences. She was completely self-assured, secure in her own skin, in any situation, and with any group. What I learned from her was one of the most valuable lessons of my life. Could I ever drop my own insecurities and develop that kind of self-confidence? Stephanie, I thought, might teach me how.

I broke the tension by asking her to dance. Stephanie looked like a professional go-go dancer from an Elvis Presley movie; I looked more like the robot from the TV series *Lost in Space*.

After a few uncomfortable dances we took a much-needed break, and I led her to the big crystal bowl of Hawaiian Punch sitting on a lunch table in the rear of the gym. As we walked up, I noticed my English teacher, Mr. Watson, standing behind the refreshment table. He obviously had agreed to be a chaperone for the evening and was forcing a smile on all of the young dance attendees who surrounded him.

He acted glad to see me, but even more glad to meet Stephanie. I introduced them and they seemed to hit it off after Mr. Watson asked about her major, as he had also done his undergrad work at Cal State Fullerton. After a few minutes of listening to their elevated conversation, I realized I was now the outsider, and they had totally forgotten about me. My insecurities bloomed as Mr. Watson and Stephanie chatted easily and in complete rhythm.

I looked around and, feeling like a third wheel, I needed to escape. There was a girl standing by herself near the far exit of the gym, and something about her looked familiar. Looking more closely through the blond hair that fell onto her face, I recognized her: it was JoAnne McGuire.

JoAnne was the younger sister of Jeannie McGuire, whom my brother had dated when he was in high school. Our families knew each other, and I had seen her at various events through the years. I remembered her as a plain little girl whom I had no interest in. She was a few years younger than I was and probably a sophomore by now, I assumed. None of that mattered; she was a way out.

I should have excused myself from the conversation but neither Stephanie nor Mr. Watson would have noticed, so I simply disappeared.

"Hi, JoAnne," I began. "It's me, Steven Reilly, remember me?"

"Stevie!" she exclaimed. She squinted at me to get a better look. She was short, petite really, and I towered over her. "Gosh, I haven't seen you for years. You go to St. James, don't you?"

"Yeah, I'm going to graduate in a few months. Do you go to Marywood, or are you someone's date?"

"Both. I'm a sophomore here, but I came with a St. James guy, Bobby Rifkin."

"I know him, I have chemistry and Latin with him, football player; hangs out with that crowd."

I couldn't figure out how this plain-looking girl had wound up with a senior jock. It didn't fit, but it was piquing my curiosity. "Where is he?" I asked her.

"He's in asshole-land," she said. "This is our first date. I met him at Shakey's Pizza after the St. Paul football game. He seemed nice, and I thought it might be fun to go to the big dance with him. I had to talk my parents into letting me go and then I bought this god-awful dress to wear and got all made up. All that, and the asshole I'm with can't talk about anything but himself, and then leaves me here while he goes out to the parking lot to drink beer with his asshole friends."

"Boy, I hope I never get on your asshole list," I replied.

"You won't, unless you act like one, and I have a feeling that won't happen."

My hormonal antenna went up with that comment and I studied her with a much more critical eye.

"Do you mind?" she said, picking something out of her purse with a deft move.

Not waiting for an answer, she pulled her thick blond hair back with both hands gently and secured it behind her with a black hair clip. She was still partially hidden by the white-plastic-rimmed eyeglasses she wore, but suddenly I could see her whole face, her neck, and her shoulders, which were exposed by the pretty white dress she wore. She, or someone, had applied just enough makeup to accent her dark brown eyes and high cheekbones.

She smiled, brightly, into my eyes, and asked me, "Do I look all right?"

"Yes, fine. No, no, great. You look, --- great, would you like to dance?

"What about Miss America?"

"Oh," I choked out, "my date."

"Yeah, she's definitely the hit of the party. Every guy here, including the idiot I'm with, has been drooling over her. Is she actually your date, or did you volunteer to bring a chaperone with you?"

"She's my date, but she's occupied with an older man right now. I would really like to dance with you, not her."

She smiled at the comment; "OK then, I can try and make her jealous."

We danced a few fast dances at first. Jack, meanwhile, was showing off by beating the crap out of his drums on "Little Latin Lupe Lu" by the Righteous Brothers. JoAnne was a very considerate dancer. She stayed close to me, occasionally grabbing my hand and helping me move around. I felt much more at ease with her than I did with Stephanie. I even started to enjoy dancing, something that had never crossed my mind before.

Easily moving from the Rolling Stones to Dick Dale and the Del-Tones, the band finally landed on the Beach Boys' "Surfer Girl," a dreaded "slow" song.

I put my sweaty palms around JoAnne's waist and gave it a try. After a few steps, I knew that she knew, that I did not know, how to slow dance. I also realized, however, that she didn't care. She drew closer to me, set me at ease, and began the "slow dance shuffle." It was a miracle! A revelation! All I had to do to be an expert dancer was shuffle my feet and turn in slow circles. We were dancing as one, and my self-consciousness melted away. Her eyeglasses were bothering me as they kept hitting my shoulder when she came close to me. It happened once, twice, and the third time I looked at her and took them off with both hands. I folded them and put them in my pocket. I examined her face again, this time more closely.

Boy, I thought. *This just keeps getting better.*

She began to talk to me, quietly, conversationally, asking me questions, and I answered them. I asked her questions, and she answered back. I looked around. We were alone, dancing, talking; the music had stopped.

Something was missing. It was my shyness. My ineptness. Where had it gone? This girl had found it, and magically made it disappear.

"You're ignoring Miss America," she said at last. "She is your date, you know. Also, I think I need to find a ride home, and it's sure not going to be with you."

"No, you're right," I replied. "I have an obligation here. I better go. My friend Jack has a ride back with his buddy in the band, and I think he is almost done playing. How about he gives you a ride home? I think I can trust him."

"Would you mind?" she said. "I think my friend is passed out drunk somewhere."

"Look," I said. "That was nice. I mean, really nice. Do you think your parents would let you go out on a date with me? I mean, just you and me?"

"Well, I think my parents would approve, but really, Steven, it's my decision, isn't it?"

I held my breath.

"Of course, silly, call me. You got lucky tonight. You were competing with an asshole."

We laughed; she kissed me on the cheek and said good night.

I pointed her out to Jack, and he agreed to take her home with his friend. He was puzzled at the turn of events, but I was in no mood to fill him in on the details.

Stephanie was sitting in a chair, alone, by the exit. She had been asked to dance many times but had refused on the shaky grounds that she had a date. I didn't have to say anything to her; we just left.

*****

It took a while as we drove home, but she spoke first, with just the slightest hint of sarcasm. "I like that girl you were dancing with. She was pretty, and you two looked good together."

"She's just a friend," I replied. "I knew her years ago. My brother dated her older sister. I hadn't seen her in a while and it was good to get caught up. Just a friend that's all."

"I see, a friend. I've *seen* friends dance together, Steven. Friends don't dance like that, do they? If she's a friend, what does that make me?"

"*You're* my date. You would be my girlfriend if it was up to me."

"Steven," she replied, "I've learned one important thing in college:

clarity. It's a gift. Let me give you that gift: *that* girl will be more than a friend. I could see the chemistry between you two from the back of the room. I would bet you have never talked to anyone that much, let alone a girl. *She* should be your girlfriend. I," she continued, "I am the friend. The one you call when you are having girl problems. The one you call at the last minute to go out with because your date got sick. When you go to college and you have problems with a professor, you call me. I like you. You're an honest, hard-working kid, and you treat my uncle very well. We could be very good *friends.*"

She couldn't have been more clear, and she was right, it *was* a gift. I didn't want to admit defeat, but I knew she was right.

"You and Mr. Watson hit it off pretty good," I said. "I'm sorry I took off, but you two were deep in conversation and I felt left out."

"That's fine, Steven, we had a lot to talk about. He went to the same school as I do and he had the same major. Fascinating man, really. He thinks you're a great student, by the way. Loves your writing."

"English lit, my only scholastic highlight. Would you date him? He's single, you know."

"No, definitely not. I know his type; he's too set in his ways. I made a rule a long time ago never to date anyone who wears a bow tie. You know, Steven, despite the fact that you almost killed me on the way to the dance, that you brought your friend along who is really strange and had a big drum with him, that you left me and found another girl to dance with, and that you were dancing with her very romantically right in front of me, I had a *really* good time tonight."

Once that all soaked in, we both broke out laughing. We laughed so long and hard we started to cry. We were still laughing when we got to her apartment.

I circled around and opened her door. She popped out of the Caddy, looked me right in the eyes, and said, "I meant what I said. Let's be friends, OK?"

She pulled me close to her and gave me a big luscious kiss on the lips, long enough to tantalize, but short enough to be friendly instead of romantic. Before I could agree with her proposition she was gone, and the only sound was of the front door closing behind her.

I had a lot to reflect on during the drive home. What would a friendship with Stephanie be like, and what was my next move with JoAnne? How could I tell my father I'd nearly wrecked the Caddy and destroyed the suspension?

It turned out I never spoke to Pop about the car and I was off the hook. From what I heard, the mechanic at Doug Schultz gave him the bad news and he apparently forgot about lending me the car and assumed it was he who had done all the damage to it in a fog of alcohol. I let the sleeping dog lie.

One thought, however, kept intruding on the others. It was Jack's hundred-dollar bill. Why would the Roach care about me? Did he think I could cough up the money for Herb? I hadn't the slightest idea how much he owed or how this whole bookie thing worked. It worried me. I was now snarled up in this rat's nest Herb had crafted, and it might be tricky getting out.

Chapter Twenty-Three

THE DEBT

Monday brought new reflections on both JoAnne and Herb. I was excited about the prospect getting to know JoAnne, but I was also worried about Herb. I went to work after school as usual and discovered that we had two cars in need of delivery that night. I wanted desperately to talk to Herb about the date with Stephanie and how it had turned out, but it would have to wait until the drive home, as we were in separate cars on the way up.

Herb looked especially nervous that night, and I noticed that even Speed looked somewhat on edge. I spotted Speed using his bony finger to motion Herb into the back corner of the old garage for a secretive meeting between the two of them and wondered what was going on. I finished inspecting the 1960 silver Oldsmobile 88 I was going to deliver and walked back to break up the conversation the two were having and tell Herb I was ready to leave.

"Speed say this Chevy here ain't done, Chief," Herb told me. "Ah kin take the Olds up an' git the otha car at Schultz. You stay here an' help Speed finish this here car and we kin take it back tomorra."

Before I could answer, he had spun around and sprinted over to the Oldsmobile. He jumped in and sped off.

Speed looked at me and just shrugged his shoulders. "Guess he's in a hurry-up, Mista Steven," he said. "You don' need to help Speed. Ah finish this one here. You work inna office if you want. Payday tomorra, bes' get ready, Herb need his pay this week."

I thought it odd he cared about Herb's pay more than his own, but I didn't argue. I went directly into the office; it was cold in there, colder than it should have been. I turned on the old portable electric heater that belonged to Speed. He'd found it in a trashcan behind the shop and repaired the broken plug it had been thrown out for. It wasn't very reliable, or safe, and it did not help with the chill I was feeling that day.

Andy and his family finished up early and went home around four thirty. It was just Speed and I there at about five. Speed was polishing the chrome on an old Chevy and I was tallying up the jobs everyone had worked on that week in order to issue payroll the next day.

A bright light reflected in my window as I sat at my desk and it blinded me for a moment. I stood and looked outside. The headlights pulled up and stopped close to the street corner. The lights went out, and then I could see; it was the Roach.

I wasn't in the mood to make excuses. I figured he could go talk to Speed and I would stay in the office, out of sight. Herb and I needed to talk this out, and soon. I didn't like the guy, and I didn't like his ominous cloud that was always hanging over us.

He passed right by Speed and came to the door of the office. He held his hand to his forehead and looked through the window to see if I was there. I could see his malevolent face clearly through the glass. The door opened and he let himself in.

"Mr. Steven!" he exclaimed with a wicked smile. "Or should I call you *Chief*?"

"Steven is good," I answered. "What can I do for you, Mr. Roché?"

"Eddie, Eddie is just fine. Mind if I sit down?"

I sensed that he was up to something, and this would not be your typical visit.

"Sure, pull up a chair. What can I do for you Mr.—uh, Eddie?"

The Roach slid a chair out from the corner of the little office and sat in it backwards, but facing me, only a few feet away. He looked his usual slick self tonight; there was a black leather jacket covering a vest with a crisp white shirt underneath it all. Maybe it was the vest, but I thought he looked heavier than usual.

He tipped the chair forward, his face then only a few feet from mine. I fixated on his pencil-thin mustache as it manipulated his unlit stogie around with his words. "You know, boy, 'scuse me, *Steven*. Yo' friend Herb has got himself in some trouble. Do you know what kinda trouble?"

"Well, if it has to do with you, Eddie, its got to be money trouble. One thing you have wrong, though, Herb is my employee, not my friend."

I felt badly after I said it, but I had to consider who I was dealing with.

"Now, *Steven*, Ah know that ain't exactly true. Maybe Herb ain't *your* friend, but you shore is *his*. He thinks a lot of you, boy. Don't know why he took a skinny white boy under his wing, but he shore did."

His slang was not as severe as I was used to, and he didn't have much of an accent. I thought his diction more schooled than street-learned.

"Now you see, *Steven*," he continued, "you and me got a *problem*. This man, the one that's not a friend a yours, he run up a big tab, an' he ain't payin' it. Long ago his credit run out. I been a patient man, Steven, but time's up. He got to pay the piper, and the piper is me."

"How is that my problem, Eddie? It's not my debt, it's Herb's."

"Cause," he said, "*Ah* say so."

I looked down; there was a pool of sweaty condensation forming on the desk. It came from my hands that were resting on it.

"How much are we talking about, Eddie? I can take a little out of his paycheck each week. I can even loan him a few hundred for a while up front. Can't we work something out?"

"Eighty-five hundred dollars."

"Eighty-five!" I yelled out. "How could he possibly owe that much money?"

"How many times I been here and you tol' me he was gone, Steven? Each week that money, it rolls over, he bets more, he lose more. Then, then they is the interest. You know, I got ta make interest if I loan him the money. Eighty-five hundred large, *Chief*, and I want it *now*."

"Look, I, Herb, or any of us around here can't come up with that kind of money, Eddie. You know that. You're wasting your time trying to collect it all at one time."

"I think Herb is a man that can *get* that kind of money. He has friends, and God knows he has a silver tongue. He gonna get that money and give it to me, tonight. What he *really* needs is a *motivation*. Amazin' what a man can do when he is *mo-ti-vat-ed*."

"Well, what did you have in mind?" I said, not wanting to know the answer.

"Well, Steven, that's something I think we should discuss. Just you and me Steven; men, lookin' for a motivation. You like *meatloaf*, Steven?"

"Meatloaf?"

"Yeah, meatloaf. Your momma made meatloaf, didn't she, Steven? You like it or not?"

"Yeah, it's OK, I guess."

"Tina makes the best meatloaf in the county, Steven. Ah *love's* Tina's meatloaf. Le's you an' me go on down to Tina's Diner and get us some meatloaf. Two men, eatin' meatloaf, discussin' what motivates another man. Whatta ya say, Steven? Meatloaf?"

"Nah," I told him, "not really hungry, Eddie, I think I oughta go home now. My mom might get worried."

"Aw, she won't care. You a grown man, got your own business, come and go as you please. Ah think you and me gonna go get us some meatloaf."

And with that, he pulled his vest open just enough to expose a brown leather holster that held what looked like a real live pistol.

Now, I had seen plenty of toy guns in my time, but never a real one. Hunting and gathering were not exactly on our family crest. If we'd had a crest, it would have shown a briefcase below an open mouth that symbolized the long lineage of salesmen who were handed down to me.

It was big. It was no popgun, and it *was* real.

With that he stood up, smiled out of character, and opened the door for me. I did as I was told and walked in front of him on the way to his car. He opened the passenger door for me.

"Get in," he said.

As I got in, I looked back at Speed. His head barely stuck out over the top of the Chevy, but he was looking at us. At least I knew someone had witnessed my predicament.

*****

Tina's Diner was on the same street as my shop, about a mile down the road. It was a classic oval-shaped diner that had been around forever and looked its age. The neon sign that said "*DINER*" had always remained the same, but the hand-painted portion in front of it that spelled out "*Tina's*" had changed many times over the years.

Tina was a large, loud, rude, just-past-middle-age woman who ran a tight ship. She had no time for loud customers, rude customers, customers who weren't sure what to order, or, worst of all, customers who wanted the food cooked their way. She also had one rule for hiring waitresses: they had to look and act just like her. You didn't go to Tina's for a cheerful, pretty, young waitress. What you did go there for was the food.

Years ago Tina had hired a cook, known to everyone only as Bean. Bean was a good-looking young black man who at the time had just gotten out of the navy. Tina was smart enough to recognize Bean's extraordinary gastronomical skills and made him a partner in her little cafe. They made a great team, and despite Tina's efforts to drive customers away, people came from all over for the food.

The Roach led me to a greasy, white Formica table in the far corner of the diner. Tina was working that night; she poured two cups of coffee without being asked.

"Eddie," she greeted us, "a little early for ya, ain't it? Stevie, --- a little late for ya, ain't it?"

Tina knew me; I had been going there since I was a kid and recently I would come and pick up sandwiches for everyone at the shop. Everyone loved Bean's corned beef sandwiches.

Eddie answered for both of us.

"Bus-ness meetin'. You know, Tina, this young man here owns his own business. You got to *respect* that. Jest like you, Tina; *business* owner. Got a nice ring to it, don't it?"

"Only thing I respect, Eddie, is your order," she replied as only Tina could. "Whaddya ya want?"

"Why Tina, Bean's special meatloaf, of course." – Bean took a slice of meatloaf and fried it on the griddle in bacon grease until it was crusty on the outside, that's what made it so special. – "Make that two, and Tina, hurry-up. The boy here is hungry."

"I ain't hurryin' for him or nobody else, Eddie," she yelled out so everyone in the diner could hear and not make the same mistake. "When Bean gets it ready, that's when it's ready."

"You my special girl, Tina. Don't really care for the food here. Come for the service."

She huffed and puffed and walked away.

We both took a sip of the dirty brown coffee and looked at each other trying to decide who would speak first.

I did; "So, you think Herb is gonna miraculously come up with the money if you threaten me?"

"Maybe. Herb likes you. My bet, he not gonna let anything happen to you if he can help it, an' I think he can help it."

"Think you're wrong on both counts, Eddie. Can't imagine he can come up with the money, and really, I'm not like family, I'm just the guy he works for."

My face betrayed me; he knew that wasn't true.

"Ah know Herb got a pretty wife an' a cute little daughter, but ya see, Ah'm a fam'ly man maself. Fam'ly is always last resort. Not saying Ah rule it out, just last resort. Speakin' a which, you got fam'ly, Steven, you know what it's like. Nice fam'ly ova there in Fullerton. Sycamore, that's a nice street, nice place to grow up with your fam'ly. No matter all that, Ah think you is goin' to do the trick. You the next best thing to fam'ly."

I was considering my options now. I could run; he would never hurt me in a crowded place. Or I could go to the bathroom and try to slip out the back. Those options, however, wouldn't solve the problem. He knew where I lived, and he knew about Herb's family. I could go to the police, but I couldn't prove anything and I wasn't sure which side of the law Herb was sitting on right now. My only option was to try and talk my way out of it.

"What exactly is your business, Eddie?" I asked him. "Is it taking illegal bets on horse racing? Are you a bookie?"

"Naw, naw, you got me all wrong. I'm a businessman, like you. You sell a product or give a service to people that need it, and, maybe, you make a profit. My product is money. I lend money to people that need it. What they use it for is their business. Herb, he uses it to bet on the ponies. He might just as well buy groceries with it, but he don't. He bets on the ponies."

"But you take bets on those ponies, that's a bookie."

"Naw, wrong again. Ah just takes Herb's order and gives it to the man. Then I cover Herb's bet. Ah just doin' what my customer needs done. My money comes from in-terest. You borrow money you got to pay in-terest. You know all them banks you drive by every day? Ah'm jest another bank, that's all, Steven. An honest businessman, just like you."

"Yeah, well, I don't carry around a gun and threaten people. Neither do the banks, Eddie."

"Oh, you wrong, boy. Them banks, they threaten people every day. They threaten to take *homes* away, leave a man homeless, take his furniture, everything he got. See, I cain't take all that. Ah got to use per-suasion instead. Like I said, motivation is the key here to success. Ah'm motivated to put a hurt on someone if'n Ah don't get my money; Herb, he be motivated to get the money if he know that. Business, Steven, business, just like yours."

The meatloaf arrived; Tina threw it on the table in front of us, saying nothing. She then took a well-worn ketchup-stained rag out of her apron pocket and began to wipe the French fry grease and spilled 7 Up off of the table next to us. Her head tilted towards us; she was eavesdropping on our conversation. Was it curiosity, or was she worried about me? Would she help? I couldn't tell.

She shuffled awkwardly back to our table.

"Well," she said, "did you two businessmen agree on anything?"

"Yeah," the Roach replied, "we certainly did." He smiled at her, that rare, thin, evil smile of his.

She filled our cups and looked into my eyes.

"Is *your* business---all right, Stevie?"

The Roach stared right through me.

"Yeah, it's all right, Tina," I told her. "Everything's OK."

She was suspicious, but she turned and left us alone.

The meatloaf was tasty, but I couldn't eat any. My stomach was in as much turmoil as my mind. I was pretty good at figuring things out, but this was out of my league. Herb was the only one who could get us out of this, and I had no idea where he was.

"You know, Eddie," I said, "I can't tell ya where Herb is or how to get a hold of him."

"Not a problem, son, Speed knows where he is. We're gonna meet him at eight o'clock. He'll have the money."

He had this all planned out. It was out of my control now; I could only hope this ended well and Herb would come through somehow. The Roach then pulled out a fat roll of twenty-dollar bills and paid the check at about a quarter to eight.

"Let's go," he said.

We drove in silence; there was little else for me to say. He pulled the Caddy into the driveway of the shop. A dim light was shining in the office.

The Roach followed me as we walked over and found Herb sitting in my chair behind the desk. He looked tired, very tired. Hard work could wear him out, but not like this. He looked up at me with big sad eyes.

"Herb," I called out to him, "man, am I glad to see you! You need to make a deal here and get us outta this."

"Steven," he said slowly, "Ah'm so sorry. Didn't know would come ta this. Didn't know the nasty low-down son-bitch Ah was dealin' with."

He wouldn't look at the Roach, only at me.

The Roach wasted no time. "Got the money, Herb?"

"Naw," he replied, "Ah tried. Ah really did. Ah went afta ever'body Ah know. Even called some women I shouldn't a. I got three hunert dollars and I give yah half my paychecks till it's paid, but they ain't no way nohow I got, nor can git, that kinda cash raght now."

"Half paychecks!" Roach yelled at him. "It would take you ten years to pay me off. I warned you, Herb. I warned you about them ponies. You done brought this on yourself, and what one brings on hisself he brings on his fam'ly and his friends. I done told you to borrow that money. You got fam'ly back east, you coulda got it from them."

"Nosah," Herb replied, "tha's ma wafe's fam'ly, done burned that bridge long tame ago. They give me nothin', an Ah don' blame em. My fam'ly, they all dead'n gone away. No suh, jes the 'Erb. This boy ain't got no money, my frens ain't got no money, an I sure ain't got nothin's worth nothin'. You got ta do to me what you got to do, Eddie, but you leave this heah boy outta this. This betwixt you an' me."

"No, Herb, you ain't gettin' off that easy. I told you a long time ago, you bet with me, the stakes be high, you, your family, and ever'body you know. You ain't gettin' off with no second-class beatin'. That's jest too easy."

Now I was worried. We were at an impasse. Somehow I'd thought Herb would come up with part of the money and talk his way out of the rest. That wasn't going to happen; it was now the Roach's move.

"You made this nasty bed, Herb," he said. "Now you gotta sleep in it. I tell you what. I'm thinking you kin do better. How 'bout I let the boy stay with me tonight and you get the cash tomorrow. You don't have the money tomorrow, the boy and I go visit that nice wife a yours and we all have a little talk. One day, Herb; then you right about one thing, *Ah got to do what Ah got to do.*"

Herb's head was in his hands, hiding his face. His chin was wet from the few tears that made it through his fingers.

"Please, Eddie, Ah'm beggin' ya, tell me somethin' Ah kin do ta make it raght, but let the boy go. Ya got ta let him go an' leave my faml'y alone. Ain't *raght*, jest ain't raght."

"No, Herb, twenty-four hours, that's it. Let's go, boy."

My heart was racing now. It was crazy to think I could go with him, but I had to.

He put his hand inside his vest.

"You hear me, boy, le's go!"

Suddenly, the passage door from the office to the shop exploded open with a loud bang. The Roach and I flinched backward, away from the explosion. There, staring at us, was Andy. Speed had gone to his house and given him the heads-up. He had sneaked into the back of the shop and kicked the office door open in order to surprise the Roach. Cradled in his arms was a rusty old double-barreled shotgun that he now had pointed at the Roach's head. Randy and Sandy stood behind him on either side, pointing a couple of twenty-two-caliber rabbit guns in the same direction.

"Best put thet handgun o' yor'n on the desk there, Eddie," Andy said. "Don't try nothin', Ah shot a man afore an' Ah'll do it ag'in if it comes to thet. Jest cleaned the old scattergun yestaday, works jes fane, it do, jest in case you curious."

The Roach did not change his expression; he seemed to accept his fate. He gently pulled the revolver out of its holster and laid it on the desk. Andy nodded to Randy, who came over and retrieved it. When the gun was safely tucked away, Andy gave the shotgun to Sandy, leaving the two boys to stand guard.

"Maybe you got me now," the Roach said, "but that don't change the situation. We still got a problem, and it ain't goin' away."

"Thet could be true, sir, but Ah sees it diff-rent. Now, you got a bone ta pick with Herb here, I unnerstan'. He owes you money; he got ta figger out how's ta pay it back. This here boy, howsomever, ain't got no debt to you, and ain't done nothin' to you. You settle with Herb, you leave the boy out of it."

"I can always get to the boy, Calhoun, if I want to,"

"Wail, now there's truth to thet, Eddie, but like Ah said, the boy done nothin' wrong. Now, we a fair people, us Calhouns, you be fair with us, we be fair with you. Boy here, he ain't fair, an' us forty-three

Calhouns all look out for what's fair and what ain't, if'n you see what Ah mean."

The Roach thought about that for a minute before he came up with his answer. "All right, Calhoun, the boy stays out of it." He turned to Herb. "That doesn't change our deal, Herb; I want the money tomorrow. I have other ways to collect."

He turned to leave, then turned once more, back to Andy. "My gun," he said.

Andy nodded at Sandy. Sandy took the gun, popped it open, dumped the bullets on the floor, and then handed it back to the Roach. I had the feeling the boys had done this before.

The black Caddy screeched off in a cloud of Roach's nasty dust; it was over.

Herb sat back in the chair and let out a big sigh.

"Andy, you done saved us," he said, "Ah don' know how ta thank ya. That Roach, he a *dangerous* man."

"Ah saved the boy," Andy replied, "but yo' ass is a still a hangin' out the kitchen window. You got a one-day re-prieve, partner. Ah don' know how ya gonna git thet money, but ya better git it. Ah cain't pro-tect you an' yer fam'ly too. You got to figger somethin' out."

Herb was ashen-faced as he thought through the consequences. He'd always had the right answer, until now.

"What are you going to do?" I asked him.

"Ah don' know," he replied. "Ah'll think o' somethin'. Ah got a day ta save my fam'ly somehow, thet's what I got ta do."

"Herb," Andy said, "we can pull together 'bout a thousand, if thet helps."

"I think I can get together a few hundred if I borrow some from my dad," I put in.

"You men," Herb replied, "all; you great frens. I thank you, but this a big *de*-cision. I got to figure out how to end this thang or the Roach be aroun' a corner looking fo' me an' ma fam'ly the rest o' ma lafe. Ah let you all know tommora what is the plan. Le's go home now, I got some figurin' out to do."

Chapter Twenty-Four

THE NEWS

The weather was as dreary as the mood I was in. An unusually violent winter storm had blown in over the weekend. They called it El Niño, but it felt more like an evil omen swirling around me.

No one saw or heard from Herb on Tuesday, but then again, we didn't really expect to. School on Wednesday played out in slow motion. It was a two-slap-on-the-head day for Father O'Brien, as all I could think about was getting to the shop and talking out Herb's dilemma with him.

"You want I drive for ya today?" Jack asked at the bell.

"Yeah," I replied, "you can ride over with me." I wasn't sure I needed him to deliver cars, but I thought he might come in handy, depending on Herb's plan.

Neither of us spoke on the way to the shop. Jack could tell I was in an ugly mood and knew better than to try and pry me out of it. We pulled into the shop and I looked around. The Calhouns were all working, but something seemed amiss. No one looked at us, or even acknowledged that we were there. Andy was painting the engine on a 1964 Jeep Wagoneer. He poked his head out sideways from under the hood, glanced at me with a dead face, and then went back to his work.

I was in no mood to ask what was going on, so Jack and I headed to the office and sat down. I pulled out my work sheet to see what cars needed to be delivered for the day.

"Where's Herb and Speed?" Jack asked me.

"Hell, I don't know. Chances are Speed's at the coffee shop and Herb is probably hiding somewhere. I don't know how I got involved with all the problems these guys have. They got nothin' to do with me. Sometimes I feel like a babysitter. All I do is listen to who is sick in the Calhoun family, or why they need more money. Speed falls asleep with a buffer in his hands and Herb has to hide out from gun-toting bookies. Shit, I was almost in the middle of a shootout! What the hell did I do to deserve all this grief? These people aren't my family, for God's sake, they're just a bunch of half-assed workers tryin' to take as much money from me as they can."

I turned to Jack. He had left. I was talking to myself.

I walked out into the shop where Jack and Andy were deep in conversation. They both looked serious, Jack listening intently; neither of them would look at me. I was in no mood to play games so I walked back into the office and sat down. Out of the corner of my eye I saw Speed's car pull up to the curb. Speed eased himself out of his old Cadillac at, even for him, an unusually slow pace. He walked straight to the office, and to me. There was a flimsy cardboard holder in his hands holding two large cups of Winkle's coffee, lids on both. He had his usual black coast guard captain's hat on to protect his head from the rain, but he was still pretty moist by the time he got to me.

He struggled to open the door while juggling the hot coffee. I could have helped him, but I didn't. At last he edged in, rear end first, turned, and put the coffee on the table. He sat without a greeting, backwards, on a chair facing me. Speed looked only at the coffee, not at me, while sugaring both cups. Finally he finished and pushed one of the cups across the table. I saw Andy and Jack outside, through the cracked-open passage door to the shop. They were looking toward the office, not saying a word. My focus was on Speed, not on them.

"What's up Dave?" I called him by his proper name, it just seemed right. "Where's Herb? What's the plan?"

At last he looked up at me, into my eyes. His were big, brown, rheumy pools of old age, older now, much older than I remembered them. His face was wet, but not all from the rain.

"'Erb's daid," he said, now no more than a few inches from my face. "He done hung hisself. Monday naght. Ah shoulda been wit him, Ah shoulda stop him, but Ah din' thank he could do it. He tol' me he hadda do somethin' drastic kinda. Ah thought he run, Ah dadn't thank he would kill hisself, but he daid."

It was an emotion I now too often identify with, but did not then. As we grow older and lose loved ones, it becomes sadly familiar. I was, however, only seventeen years old. It was a cattle prod up my ass; a fuzzy headache, an artificial feeling, like watching a sad movie that you knew just couldn't really be true.

"No, no," I mumbled. "I have some money to give him, so does Andy. Let's just give him the money, that's all. Speed, it's only money."

"He daid, Mista Steven." He said it loud and clear as he tried to get through the thick fog I was lost in. "You got to face it, son, he daid. He daid 'cause he love his fam'ly and seen no way out. 'Erb love his fam'ly mo' than hisself. Don' want nothin' to hurt his fam'ly, onliest way he figured was to make the 'Erb be gone, fer good."

"What about Lizzie? And the baby?"

"She done gone a'ready. When she foun' him, she know why he done it 'cause he done left a note. She pack up the chile and take the bus to Chee-ca-go, las' naght it was. She gonna go back to her folks. I ain't supposed to know that, so don' tell the Roach nothin'. Ah thank the Roach leaves her alone now. Ain't her money ta owe, an' he ain't gonna chase no one that far 'less it be the 'Erb hisself."

I was trying to assimilate all this information and make sense out of it. Logic was having a nasty fistfight with my emotions, and the emotions were slowly winning out.

"When you say *fam'ly*, you mean Lizzie and the baby?"

"Course, they no one else."

"To look out for, I mean."

"Only faml'y; Lizzie, an' the chile."

I would not let him look away.

"Suuure, he worry 'bout you too, son, you his bes' fren somehow. He kill hisself fer his fam'ly, though, not fer you, boy. You a man, he figures you take care a youself now. Ah thank he figures he teaches you 'nuff, you kin make it through bad tames, through Roaches an his kine, an him dyin' too. Naw, he daid 'cause a his fam'ly, you got nothin' to do with what happen, son."

My head felt heavy, swollen, as it dropped down into my hands. It was beginning to sink in. My eyes moistened, but no one had ever taught me how to cry, so I simply hid my face and talked through my fingers.

"You don't know; he's my *friend*. He can't be here one day and gone the next. Herb, he's the only *real* friend I have. That *son of a bitch*! He can't take his own life! He's got no right. Where in the fuck was everybody? I told you we could get the money up somehow. I don't understand any of this, it makes no sense."

There was to be no acceptance, at least not yet.

"Son, there wasn't gonna be enough money. Now Ah'm gonna miss him as much as you, but fact is, he done what he thought he had ta do. It's done, an we gonna hafta get on with it. Now you take Mista Jack home with ya. Ah get the cars de-livered tanaght, and you thank about how the 'Erb would want you ta figure this t'ing out."

He got up and left the room, quickly, as quickly as I had ever seen him move. Jack was sitting in my car with his head down in both hands. As I walked over to him I stopped and looked down at the dirty gray asphalt beneath me, and then I looked up at the sky. They looked the same, and I became dizzy and disoriented. Wet, fat raindrops burst onto my face and mingled with my tears as I was taught my very first lesson on how to cry, and who was important enough to cry for.

I was still just a kid, yet my partner, my mentor, my best friend, was dead.

I got in the car and slammed the door behind me. Jack was slumped over in his seat. He wouldn't look at me. I put the key in the ignition, but then spotted something on the dashboard out of the corner of my eye. Sitting on the perforated metal grille that held the radio speaker in the middle of the dashboard sat a crumpled up one-hundred-dollar bill.

Jack turned his face to me. He was sobbing; fat tears rolled off of his chin.

"I di'n't know, man," he babbled. "I di'n't know what would happen. I was gonna give it back to the Roach, I *was*. I'm sorry, man, I di'n't know nothin' like this could happen, man. It's the Roach, man, it's his fault."

"It wasn't your fault, Jack," I told him, "and it wasn't the Roach's. It wouldn't have mattered. He killed himself and he didn't have to. If it was anybody's fault it was mine. He was protecting me and I shoulda known something bad was gonna happen. It ain't your fault, Jack."

"Fuck, Stevie," Jack spit out through his tears.

"Fuuuuuck!" I screamed out for the whole world to hear.

The hundred lay on the dash. Neither of us would touch it.

EPILOGUE

That spring brought balmier weather, and for me, a new perspective on things. The Calhoun family became harder to control, and, really, my heart wasn't in the business anymore without Herb. Speed moved on, to where I never knew, but I missed him, and I really missed Herb. Andy seemed bitter; I think he felt partly responsible for Herb's demise, but then again, we all did. Randy and Sandy, who had since quit school to work full time, made me an offer to buy the business on behalf of the entire family. I gladly accepted the five hundred in cash plus Sandy's 1961 Ford Falcon, which I quickly sold to Larry Cheatly for an additional two hundred, in exchange for my equipment and client list. My plan was to get a full-time job in the summer selling cars for Larry at Lance-A-Lot and then take enough classes in the fall at the local junior college to avoid the draft.

Graduation was last on the list of my concerns, but all of a sudden it was forced upon me. A clear spring day shrouded the St. James gymnasium as I stood in line next to my friend Jack, waiting for our diplomas. I wondered what would become of our friendship now without the foundation of high school to keep us together.

Father Ryan had agreed to let Jack grow his hair out if he kept it trimmed properly, and he actually looked pretty good in his black cap and gown. I knew he didn't want to go to college, even though I had tried to talk him into it. He was a musician, he said, and wanted to see where that would take him. It took him, as it turned out, to the draft board, and the war, where he promptly lost the use of his right arm in a mine explosion. He landed in Las Vegas many years ago and now lives off of government disability. We communicate on Facebook occasionally, but I haven't seen him in a long, long time.

The ceremony was all a haze to me; I was distracted and unfocused. I remember nothing except empty words spoken about all the great things we were going to accomplish. That might have meant something to the boys going on to big-name colleges, but it offered nothing to me. I do remember that Father Ryan failed to mention in his speech how to sell more cars for Larry, or how to rent an apartment and get out of my parents' house, or how to forget about what had happened to Herb.

As we paraded out of the gymnasium to "Pomp and Circumstance," diplomas in hand, I scanned the crowd looking for familiar faces. In the last row on the left were my mother, smiling her posed, movie star smile, and my father, looking very stern. Next to him were JoAnne, my grandparents, Uncle Dan, and Inga; they were the only ones I really cared about being there.

Stephanie had been right about JoAnne: she had become my girlfriend. She was the one I had found, after Herb, whom I could talk to about anything. She was blunt and bold, and never failed to bring me out of my shell. I was beginning to think I was in love, but I hadn't yet defined what that word really meant. She made the day a special occasion when, to me, it should not have been one. She smiled at me as I walked by, not sweetly, but knowingly, as she was the only one who knew exactly how I felt that day.

Outside on the gym veranda the families and friends of the graduates gathered around. Jack and I hugged each other for the last time and then he left me to find his parents. JoAnne and my family found me there alone and gathered around me in a circle in order to congratulate me. I shook hands with Uncle Dan and hugged Inga, both with a genuine affection. Grandpa replaced the Camel cigarette he was holding with my hand and pumped it vigorously while Grandma pecked me on the cheek. JoAnne gave me a reassuring hug that warmed me. Mom gave me a light hug and whispered congratulations into my ear, but I was cold to her touch. My father looked at me sternly.

"Well, what the hell are you going to do now? Become cannon fodder for the army?" He called out for everyone to hear.

Four years of high school and he had never asked me what my life intentions were, let alone if I wanted to attend college. In fact, the only family who had ever shown any interest in my future were Grandma and Grandpa Reilly. I realize now that was partly my fault: I kept to myself, and I lived a very independent life. I suppose my father was just never that concerned about me. He assumed, incorrectly, that I knew what I was doing and had everything all planned out. Either that or he just didn't care.

"No, Dad," I replied. "I plan to work this summer and go to Fullerton Junior College in the fall. Don't worry, though, I'll pay for it myself."

He winced. I had cut him to the quick in front of his wife, his parents, and my girlfriend, and he did not take it lightly. I felt badly, and felt even worse when I looked at a disapproving JoAnne.

I looked around, at the circle of people now trapping me in the middle of this uncomfortable gathering. I realized these were all the people, through the good and the bad, who had an impact on my life, who made me who I am. There was an empty space in the crowd, an opening in the circle; someone was missing. We all knew who it was.

I suddenly felt nauseous, claustrophobic, confined in the small circle of people around me and I needed to escape.

I broke through the crowd and veered toward the lunch area that lined the wide walkway leading to the side entrance of the school. I found, and drank from, the old lunch-place water fountain for the last time. Looking back, I saw the silver flagpole that supported the American flag in front of the school. It was shimmering brightly in the afternoon sun and it beckoned to me; I wanted to be near it one last time.

I walked between the neat rows of picnic benches on either side of the walkway that divided the upperclassmen on one side from the lower classmen on the other. We learn these divisions early, I thought to myself. They group us by age, grade point average, athletic ability, and sex. Soon we learn how we do it ourselves; clubs, cliques, race, religion, Democrat, Republican, it never stops.

Shit, I thought, I've been consigned to a group for as long as I can remember.

Was it a learned science, this selection process, or is the need to join a group in our genetic makeup? The only group I'd ever voluntarily joined was Reilly Detail: Speed, Andy, and Herb, and now they were all gone.

A sad old gnarly oak tree protected the entrance to the school that led to the flagpole. There was a bench underneath it that, I always assumed, was designed for student contemplation of a higher order. I was familiar with the bench, as I had eaten lunch there with Jack many times while attempting to avoid any social interaction with the other students. Someone was sitting there now, alone. I couldn't see the stranger's face, but I judged it was a man by the size of the coat he was wearing.

Something drew me to the mysterious person. He wore a heavy, gray pea coat; odd, I thought, as it was a warm day. There was an aura about the man, and I was drawn to it. I stood behind him, though he did not know I was there. I recognized the cap: it was Speed's old captain's hat.

"Herb?" I asked.

He turned his head slowly and looked up. A full beard and mustache, along with a pair of dark glasses, hid his face, but I knew: it was he.

"Chief; you look *nace*. Purty dress ya got on, nace hat too. *Con-grat-a-lations*, boy. Ah's proud a ya."

I was speechless; I stood there, incredulous.

"Sit down, son, talk ta me," he beckoned.

I couldn't take my eyes off him as I slid onto the bench.

"Ah know what you thinkin'," he began. "Rememba what we done talked about? Sometame a man gotta do things ain't easy ta do, but is the raght thing ta do. Sometames a man gotta pro-tect his fam'ly, pro-tect his friends. Now the 'Erb; he's daid. This here you talkin' to be Bert. Bert, he live somewheres else with his fam'ly, woikin' ha'd an getting' lots a poosy. Heh-heh-heh.

Fact is, son, Ah couldn't pro-tect Lizzie and Sarah, Ah couldn't pro-tect you. The 'Erb, he had to die, so he hung hisself. No sir, anaone ask you where the 'Erb is, he daid."

"We all chipped in!" I scolded him. "We could have made a deal with the Roach! You didn't have to leave! That was a *cowardly* thing to do! You lied and left us all out to dry, Herb."

"You gonna unnerstan' someday, Steven. Wasn't nuff money, and the Roach, he answer to a even higha powa than hisself. No, I done what I thank raght. Ah had ta save my fam'ly, save you, from somethin' Ah done. Weren't your fault; were *mane*. Man got ta take re-spon-si-bility for what he do. That's what Ah done, an it's ova now. If you learn one thing from the 'Erb, you learn you got ta do the raght thang, no matta what. Sometames it hurt. Hurt bad sometame, but it don' matta. Don' be weak, son, be strong. Do the raght thang for you'self an' do it fo' ever'one else. You do that, and you gonna be OK, you gonna be a good man. Ain't jest you son, goes fo' ever'one. You gonna teach otha men someday, jest lak Ah done teach you."

I had no reply. My mind was trying to untangle Herb's web of events while absorbing his advice. Herb, I could tell, had more to say.

"Ma daddy, he saved a white man in the foist war. Mama foun' a letta from the U-nited States givin' him a co-men-dation. Shov'lin' coal on a ship an a boiler blows up, pulls a man raght outta there. He neva said nothin' ta nobody. Thought nothin' 'bout savin' a man's lafe, he a he-ro, but to him, it was jest the raght thang to do."

I remembered back, to my grandfather's house that day.

"Was he a big man?"

"Yas, he a big man, l'arned to cook afta shovelin' coal an took cookin' jobs when he get back home."

"I think he saved my grandfather's life," I had to tell him. "I wouldn't be here if it wasn't for him. My grandfather told me the story a long time ago; he said he was a big man, the man that saved his life. He called him Tree, but he never knew his last name. He said they made him a cook's assistant. It's him. Your father saved his life."

"You don' know that, son. Lotsa men save lotsa lafes back then.

Besades, if'n he did, it was the raght thang to do, an' your gran'daddy woulda done the same thang."

My head was spinning. I wasn't sure of anything anymore. Was I talking *to* a dead man, talking *about* a dead man, or was it really Herb, alive, right here in front of me? I touched him, on the shoulder, just to make sure he was real. He took it as a sign of affection and reciprocated by holding out his big paw of a hand for me to shake.

"Ah got ta go now, Steven. Ah wonted ta say good-bye proper, wasn't raght to leave a fren lak Ah did. Ah truly proud of ya, son, ah neva see ya ag'in, but Ah wont ya ta know, 'Erb is you fren, an allas will be."

I knew he was right, that I would never see him again. I was torn between the elation of his being alive and the dread of losing him once again.

"Herb," I said as I shook his hand for the last time, "my grandfather always regretted not being able to thank your father for saving his life. I want to do that, to thank you for him, for saving his life. He would have wanted me to. Maybe he wasn't the one that did it, but if he was, I gotta thank you."

He was quiet, thoughtful, searching for answers neither of us would ever find. I thought his eyes welled up a bit. Mine were dry and serious.

"I want to thank you for being a friend too, Herb. I'm gonna miss you."

He stood, buttoned up his coat, and turned away; he was too emotional to talk.

He couldn't look at me now and his back was to me. He spoke in a sad but clear voice.

"Go to your fam'ly now, son. Fam'ly is who you need now, you see, they be there rest o' yo' lafe, good tames 'n' bad, not lak the 'Erb, not lak no one else.

Good-bye, Chief. Good-bye, Steven."

And with that he walked away.

I watched him as he faded out of sight, and then I stood up to walk slowly back to the gym, never looking back. I stopped for a moment, and gazed around the campus. I had never noticed the large parkway on either side of me that bordered the cement walkway. The grass was a vibrant green, brightened by the springtime rains. I looked up and saw the richness in the clear blue sky that was dotted with a few silvery clouds. I slid my hand down the front of my gown, and felt the silkiness of the material. A shiver ran through me, and I thought, for the very first time, that I was in control of my life, and that I knew what I had to do.

My family was still there, standing together, talking, about me I thought: this strange man-boy who could talk intimately to a stranger on a bench, but never to his own parents. I surveyed the crowd around me, and a calmness came over me. I knew I was now in command of my life.

I walked up to my mother and embraced her firmly. Then I kissed her, warmly, on the cheek.

"I love you Mom," I whispered in her ear.

I turned to my father and looked him right in the eyes, deeply, as I had never done before. I grabbed him with both arms and gave him a bear hug, trying to squeeze the love out of him that I knew was hidden, deep down inside somewhere.

"I love you Pop." I said.

I knew he could not return the sentiment. It was only on the night before he passed away, forty years later, that he would finally be able to utter those magical words.

He instead eased his shoulders back and stood up straight. A smile cracked across his stone face. He extended his hand to me. "Congratulations, Son. Good luck. I—I really *am* proud of you."

I stared at his hand for a few seconds, and then I shook it with a firm and earnest grip. It was the same grasp I had used to shake Herb's hand for the last time just a few minutes earlier.

It was not easy, but;

It was the right thing to do.

The End

ABOUT THE AUTHOR

R.P. "Rick" Heinz in 1966 with his '54 Ford

R.P. Heinz is a writer of literary fiction that is inspired by true events and the eclectic collection of people he has met throughout his interesting life.

For over forty years he worked his way through the ranks of the retail automotive business where he rose from cleaning cars at age fifteen, to owning multiple new car dealerships.

He retired from the automobile business at the age of fifty, at which time he entered college for the first time, earned his degree, and began his formal writing career. The unique relationships he has developed over the years with characters from all walks of life give his writing a genuine, and credible, tone. He resides in Newport Beach, California, and Telluride, Colorado, with his lovely wife Susan, and his faithful dog Winston.

You can find him at www.RPHeinzauthor.com.